LOVE IN A BLIZZARD

CHRISTMAS AT THE LODGE

BRITNEY M. MILLS

CRYSTAL CANYON PUBLISHING

Walker McBride hauled in the last of the wood he'd just chopped. He moved over to the wood-burning stove, adding some of the split pieces to the embers inside, causing the red to flame to life once more. The lodge was chilly because he'd let the fire die down, but it was nothing compared to the whipping wind outside.

Silver Brook Lodge sat next to Coldwater Creek on the western side of Wyoming, and at the end of November, the snow had already built up at least two feet. They were slated to get two more feet within the next few days, and Walker wanted to make sure he was prepared for it. He'd get enough questions from his family tomorrow at Thanksgiving, and he didn't need any lectures from his mother or his younger two sisters, whom his mother had trained well in the art of questioning.

His old dog, Bear, was lying on the rug next to the stove, a light snore coming from him. He'd been through a lot with that dog in the past year; there were some moments he wasn't sure whether he would have made it through all the therapies without the patience of the older animal. It seemed they were going through some of the same pains every once in a while.

Walker smiled, rubbing his hand between the dog's ears.

The phone hooked to his belt rang, and he pulled it from its holder, glancing at the screen to see it was his older brother, Easton.

"Hey, East. How are things at the ranch?" Walker poked at the new logs a few more times until the fire engulfed them. He shut the door to the stove and sat back in his favorite recliner set in the middle of the great room of the lodge. He knew he'd have to move it when the real furniture came and guests started arriving, but for now, this was his favorite spot in the place.

"Busy as always. Do you think you can stop by before we shoot tomorrow? I need some help mending that back corner fence. The cows keep getting out, and the twins, well, you know how they are." The irritation in Easton's voice caused Walker to smile. The two of them were the oldest of the six McBride siblings, and while they'd all grown up on the ranch, it seemed as though the younger ones had a somewhat different upbringing, especially his twin brothers and two sisters.

Walker looked around the lodge. "That should work. I've got everything buttoned up here for the storm. What time?"

"Dad wants to leave for shooting at seven. Do you mind coming over around five thirty?"

Blowing out a breath, Walker finally said, "Yeah, I can do that. Let's just hope it doesn't ruin our aim by being out in the cold that early. I'd hate to have one of the twins beat us again this year."

"You and me both." Easton chuckled on the other end. "I don't know if I can stand another year of them gloating over it."

The McBride men had a tradition of shooting clay

pigeons every Thanksgiving morning, and the competition was hotter than anything that happened at the local fair. It was about the only time they could get together throughout the year since there was so much to do on the family ranch and several of them had their own lives.

"I'll see you early, then. Make sure to have the road cleared for me. I'm not digging out my truck and then helping you with the fence." Walker paused, waiting for Easton's reaction.

"I'll make sure Colter gets to it. He already owes me."

Walker hung up the phone and glanced around the room once more. There were a lot of benefits to living on the ranch, but the thing he loved about this newly built lodge was that it wasn't something his parents had built from the ground up. It had been his own dream as a kid, one that he'd made a reality after retiring from bull riding. He just hoped the people of Coldwater Creek would support it as much as they'd claimed to when he bought the run-down property.

It had been sitting with eight cabins for the last fifteen years, the original lodge having burned down before that. In such a small valley, there weren't many places to eat, let alone a steakhouse, which the old lodge had included.

With only a few last-minute adjustments and fixes, the new lodge would be ready in two weeks for the chef and several of the local townsfolk he hoped to hire to help him run the restaurant and room rental. The large gathering hall behind the restaurant would be used for events and weddings, and with several more bedrooms on the upper two floors, it allowed for more family to stay in town for those events. He'd left the cabins out back, removing the old wood paneling and freshening them up with new beds and décor.

The idea to open it before Christmas had been a little crazy, but he knew people could use something different in the long hard Wyoming winters. Maybe this would be it. He'd already received two requests to rent out the large hall for family Christmas activities, and the school wanted to use it for their Christmas ball.

Looking at the clock, he realized it was nearly eleven, and his body felt it.

"Come on, boy. Let's go to bed. We've got a long day ahead of us tomorrow."

The dog rose slowly, taking one step after the other. He lumbered along faster after the first few steps as though he had to get his joints working correctly first.

They walked over to one of the two suites on the first floor, where Bear climbed onto the large four-poster bed and curled up again. He was asleep before Walker had a chance to take off his boots.

"Some company you are," Walker said, laughing a bit, the sound hollow.

As much as he claimed to people that he didn't need anyone but his dog, during a cold winter like this, he realized how much he missed having someone to talk to, someone to bounce ideas off of. Not that his former girlfriend had been all that good at the last part, but at least it wasn't silent all the time.

Pushing Cara out of his brain, he focused on brushing his teeth and changing for the night. It didn't take much as his mind went through everything that needed to be finished or fixed before guests started coming in.

Stretching out next to Bear, his mind went blank, and he was out.

CHAPTER 2

So many feelings welled up inside Lauren Burke as she got ready for the day. She wasn't sure whether to scream with excitement or cry from nerves. Today was the day. The one every little girl dreamed of, where the guy would get down on one knee and ask her to be his forever no matter what.

Well, she wasn't exactly sure of that, but one of her friends had seen her longtime boyfriend, Cory Turner, walking out of a jewelry store the day before, and with everyone gathered at his parents' home for Thanksgiving, she wondered and hoped that today would be the day.

The two of them had begun dating after she'd graduated from college three and a half years ago, and when she couldn't find a job using her art history degree, he'd offered for her to help work at his family's insurance company. It wasn't her dream job by any means, but she got to hang out with her boyfriend at work every day, or the days when he actually decided to show up before noon.

The doorbell rang, and Lauren swiped the last bit of makeup across her cheek. Straightening her shimmering gold blouse, she grabbed her heels out of the closet and walked to the door with a broad grin.

"Let me just grab my purse and coat, and I'll be ready to go."

He grunted something, glancing back down at the phone in his hand.

She made her way back to the door a few moments later and closed and locked up before she turned back to him. She buttoned her coat and waited for him to glance up. "Oh, I almost forgot," she said. "I have the stuff your mom asked me to bring. Let me run and get it."

Her boyfriend grunted again, and Lauren wondered what was up with him. He'd been really busy lately, and she hadn't been able to sit him down and ask how things were going, even though a bit of tension had settled in her stomach. But her friend's words came back to her, and she smiled, wondering if she'd be finishing the day with a call to her father to tell him she was finally engaged.

A small knot twisted inside her chest. She'd just be calling her father about one of the most important decisions of her life. Her heart ached daily to have her mother back with them again, even after four years, but it was a time like this where all she could hope for was a little reassurance that her life was finally on the right track.

She had been charged with bringing a pie to the dinner, and since she wasn't much of a cook, she'd bought and cooked one of the Marie Callender's frozen pies from the grocery store. At least no one would chip a tooth from eating it.

Balancing the pie on her hand, she moved through the door again and locked it.

Cory finally glanced up at her. He reached out to help steady her as they walked down the slippery few steps from her porch to the drive, and her worries dissipated.

Once in the car, she positioned the pie on her lap and buckled her seat belt. Cory did the same before starting the engine and pulling out of the driveway of her small townhome.

"How are things today?" she asked, glancing at him out of the corner of her eye.

He finally smiled. "It's Thanksgiving. One of my favorite holidays ever because I get all the turkey and mashed potatoes I can eat." His enthusiasm caused her to giggle.

Cory leaned forward and turned up the song on the radio, one of the first Christmas songs of the season.

"I made an apple pie for you. I hope you like it." Lauren beamed, hoping to find some line of conversation that wouldn't be over in one sentence.

Cory turned and looked down at the pie for the first time, his eyebrows mashing together in a frown. "Thanks. I've actually been craving a cherry pie for a while, though."

Cherry pie? Since when did he like cherry? He'd always liked the Dutch Apple kind with the streusel topping. It was one of her favorites as well, and the idea that he'd all of a sudden changed his mind caused a rift to split within her chest.

"I'm sure one of your sisters made one. I think your brother-in-law likes cherry, doesn't he?"

Cory grinned again. "I think you're right." He tapped along to the song on the steering wheel and asked, "Are you ready for a holiday with my family?"

Lauren sucked in a deep breath, so many emotions racing through her. "As ready as I'm going to be."

Even though they'd dated for about three and a half years, this was the first holiday they were spending together. Lauren's family thought it was crazy that they'd never met Cory in person, but it was hard to get away from the office for a drive from Colorado up to Wyoming, and his family was always on some cruise or on a beach somewhere for the holidays. This was the first time he'd asked her to come with him, and she hoped it would be the change in their relationship that would result in a forever relationship rather than the same plateau they'd been on for longer than she cared to admit.

Not that dating wasn't good, but at twenty-five years old, she was ready for the next step, for the commitment that a ring would entail. And tonight was quite possibly the beginning of that next journey.

They arrived at his parents' home, where a few inches of snow covering the front yard and the roof made it already feel like Christmas. Cory helped her out of the car, and they walked into the house, the warmth hitting Lauren like a wall. She stepped behind Cory, who walked over to kiss his mother on the cheek as she stirred something on the stove.

"Happy Thanksgiving!" he said.

His mother turned and embraced him. "You too! I've made all your favorites. We should be ready to start in about thirty minutes, so make yourself comfortable." She shooed him away, and Lauren took a step forward, holding the pie in front of her.

"Where can I put this, Sharlene?" she asked with a smile.

His mother gave her a forced smile, but that was relatively normal for their relationship. Cory was the only boy in the family, and as such, it was hard to get into his mother's good graces. Lauren often thought it strange that she wouldn't want her nearly thirty-year-old son to get married and settle down, but then again, there were a lot of things about Denver and Fort Collins that were different than where she grew up.

"The pies and desserts are on the counter in the mudroom. Just put it there if you don't mind." She turned quickly, stirring what looked like gravy in the pan. It was a bit lumpy, and the first pang of homesickness hit Lauren.

Her mother had been the best cook ever, but since her passing, the Burkes had been eating their holiday meals with their close family friends, the McBrides. Not that Lauren had actually been home much since her mother's funeral during her senior year. She'd come home for a week or two when her father had suffered a major stroke, helping to nurse him back—but her brothers all applauded Tonya McBride's cooking.

If she wanted a future with Cory, she needed to take this step and get used to dealing with his family outside the office. That's what married couples did, and she may as well come around to the idea.

After placing the pie next to the others, she went back into the kitchen. "What can I do to help? Do you need me to prepare anything or set the table?"

Sharlene turned, her eyes batting several times, making Lauren wonder if something was in them. "I think we'll be okay, Lauren. Go relax somewhere until dinner is ready."

Lauren nodded, feeling as if she'd been dismissed. It was a bit odd to not be helping out for dinner, as everyone was expected to do so in her own family.

She wandered into the living room, glancing at the large-screen television hung above the fireplace. The room was decorated with modern touches, a stark contrast to the log feel of her childhood home. Cory sat on the large couch with his sisters, all four of them lying on top of each other, staring at the TV.

Gritting her teeth, she settled into one of the chairs near the large front window. This wasn't what she'd had in mind at all.

CHAPTER 3

*W*alker could see his breath in a large cloud as he stood behind the pulling machine and loaded it with clay discs. The chill of the air was enough to make him want a hot shower and a gallon of hot chocolate. Blowing into his hands did nothing to ease the numbness, but as he listened to his brothers and dad banter back and forth, he could only smile, knowing there was nowhere else he'd rather be. Even while he'd been on the rodeo circuit, there was something about a friendly family competition that seemed to ready him for whatever came next.

Their father won for the first time in several years, and Walker had to hide a smile as he'd missed the last two targets on purpose for that reason. The man looked as though he were walking on a cloud as they trudged through the deep snow of the field back to the house.

"I saw that," Easton said a few inches from Walker's ear.

With a quick shrug, Walker smirked. "It's been a while. He needed a win."

"Well, just don't tell him that. At least not for the next ten years."

The two of them chuckled, stomping off their boots on the back porch. They took off all their snow clothes and hung them in the mudroom. It had been one of Walker's mother's biggest requests when the family had designed the house some twenty years ago. Working on a ranch meant family members coming in covered in all sorts of outdoor elements, and as a woman who liked to keep a clean house, this surely added to that order.

"Walk, will you grab me an onion from the storage room? I forgot to grab one when I went down just now." His mother squeezed his upper arm and gave him a smile.

He nodded and moved in that direction. The warmth of the house was easing into his joints and warming his fingers, causing them to sting a bit at the direct change in temperature. It didn't take long to locate the onions in his mother's labeled storage room, and he was up in the kitchen within a few minutes.

"Thank you so much, dear. How are things going with the lodge?" His mother pulled out a large knife and started slicing the onion, the smell of it hitting Walker within seconds.

"It's looking good. I just have to finish getting all the décor and furniture in. The chef I'm hoping to hire should be here next week, and then guests will come the week after. I'm hoping it fills up for Christmas."

She stopped and gave him a warm smile, always the reassuring parent. "That's wonderful, Walker. I'm so glad it's coming together so well. I was a little worried after all that happened the last year that it wouldn't—"

Walker raised a hand, not wanting to hear what she was about to say. "It'll be fine, Mom. I'm fine."

"When you're ready, there are a couple of young gals I'd love to set you up with." She winked at him, the battle over his dating life always at the surface.

"I can find my own dates, Mom. I'm just not ready for that type of a relationship yet. Not after—" He let the words trail away and nodded before moving into the living room. One of his younger brothers, Colter, stood before the wood stove, adding pieces of wood just as Walker had done the night before at the lodge.

Colter's twin, Hunter, was setting the long table with plates and utensils. There was a separate table set to the side with a plastic tablecloth.

Walker stood next to him and asked, "Why the extra table?"

"For the Burkes."

Walker had been so busy with the lodge, he hadn't really thought about their good family friends coming to dinner. They'd shared holiday meals with the Burkes over the years, and his mother was always inviting people to join them who didn't have family nearby. With the passing of Sherri Burke around four years before, it was now a tradition to have them over for holiday meals.

Walker had been best friends with Preston Burke, the oldest of the Burke family, since they were about three, both their fathers making sure they knew how to ride a horse and preparing them for the future rodeo life they'd both enjoyed.

Preston had stopped the circuit four years ago when his mother died and then his father had a stroke shortly after, paralyzing half of his body. He'd come home to take care of the dairy cows the family owned, and while he claimed he enjoyed it, the look in his eyes said he was ready for a new adventure.

Walker called up images of the rest of the Burkes: the three other brothers and then a girl who'd followed him and Preston around with wide eyes and a curiosity he'd never seen again. Lauren. For some reason, he wondered if she would show up. Not that he had any romantic interest in the younger and only sister of his best friend, but he was curious what her life had been like since she'd left Coldwater Creek for school in Colorado.

The doorbell rang, and Walker answered it, smiling wide when he saw Preston first. They slapped each other on the back, and Walker stood back to let them all in, doing what he could to help Mr. Burke up the step with his crutches.

"How's it going over there, Walk?" Preston asked, removing his cowboy hat and hanging it on one of the top hooks in the main entry.

"Progress is progress. How are the cows?"

Preston blew out a breath. "Still alive by some miracle. Adam is going to take over next week while I head out of town. I need a break from the snow and the cows. Want to come to the beach with me?" His expression held a hint of the mischievous nature Preston had always had.

Walker shook his head. "Maybe next year after the lodge has been open a few months. Right now, I need to make back some of the money I invested into getting it all running again."

With a quick slap to Walker's chest, Preston scoffed. "Please, Mr. Rodeo King. I'm sure you've still got quite the nest egg waiting for you. And it's just you. I bet you live on ramen and cereal when you don't come home for meals."

Walker rolled his eyes. "I do know how to cook, Preston. But sometimes those *are* easier than cooking a meal for one."

Hearing his mother's voice, the room quieted down as she gave instructions for the food. After a quick prayer to bless the feast laid out on the island, the group moved through the line, the mounds of food looking barely touched after the first round. His mother knew how to feed an army.

Work on a ranch stirred up an appetite, and Walker

smiled as he glanced around at the people in the room. This is what he'd missed about Coldwater Creek when he'd been on the rodeo circuit. The chance to have good friends around no matter what the weather was like outside. And to know he had a place with them, whether he was successful at life or not.

CHAPTER 4

One of the college football games was on, and even though it was normal for her family to watch them, Lauren just wasn't sure where she fit in this family. After working with them and dating Cory for so long, she kept thinking things would work themselves out, but she still felt as awkward as ever standing there.

She picked up a magazine from the table next to her chair and leafed through it. As much as she tried to concentrate on the words and pictures, her mind kept drifting to what her family would be doing right then back in Coldwater Creek. Probably taking care of the dairy cows and making sure everything was ready for the big storm she'd seen on the news. It looked like it was going to be a big one, and knowing Coldwater Creek, it would probably be near freezing until April.

"Let's eat!" Sharlene called from the kitchen. "Go ahead and serve yourselves. The food is all at the bar." She walked in with a full plate and took a seat at the table, taking a few bites as the rest of the family scrambled to fill their own plates.

Lauren was surprised at the quick reactions everyone had, each of them scrambling to find a place at the table. She watched in shock as Cory didn't even glance in her direction, acting as though she wasn't even there. A few of the girls pushed one another, trying to gain an edge in the line. Everyone stood back to allow their father ahead of them in line, the one piece of manners Lauren could get behind.

Biting her bottom lip to keep from laughing, Lauren picked up a plate at the end of the island, wondering what caused the rush. It didn't matter what the occasion was, her mother always made double the amount of food needed for their family. Feeding four growing boys was a feat, but they had always known that manners were the key to enjoying a good meal.

Lauren stood at the end of the line, disbelief seeping through her as the siblings all fought for the spoon for the potatoes or vegetables, not caring where they were in line. Maybe it was good she'd never been invited to one of the family gatherings. She and her siblings had their own little arguments, but they knew what a line meant and that there was enough food for everyone.

When she finally reached the food, there were two slices of turkey and one dollop of mashed potatoes left. The only roll in the basket looked like someone had taken a bite out of it and then put it back. Of course, the green bean bowl was still full, and it seemed the Turner family didn't care for the sweet potatoes. She filled her plate and took the only seat left on the opposite end of the table from Cory next to his dad, Curt, her boss.

There was no grace, no moments to announce what they were each grateful for. Only the sound of Cory's sixteen-year-old sister sitting across from her, smacking her lips as she chewed. Doing her best to block out the grating sound, Lauren savored the little bit of potatoes on her plate. After one bite of the turkey, she asked for the gravy to be passed down and drenched the dry meat with the lumpy sauce.

Maybe she was just being picky. Taking a breath, she told herself to keep an open mind. Just because she'd grown up with gourmet-quality food didn't mean everyone else had that chance. It wasn't like she'd had a full-course dinner for the other holidays she hadn't made it home for. But if she was supposed to spend every other holiday with these people in the future, she was going to have to lower her standards for what good food was.

"How have the sales gone this past week, Lauren?" Curt asked. He brought a napkin to his mouth and wiped, staring at her for a response.

Lauren tried to switch her brain over. She had been grateful when work was finished the day before, and once she left the office, she hadn't even thought about it. It had been so slow because of the holiday that they hadn't gotten too many new applications for Medicare. That had been their new strategy this year, on her recommendation, that they work to help current and new clients figure out which Medicare plan was right for their lives and situation, allowing them to get a commission on each one.

"Steady, I would say. There were only about three dropped off yesterday, but I think we'll see a bunch in the next week before the cutoff at the beginning of December."

Curt grinned. "Perfect. It was a great idea, by the way."

Lauren grinned at him and then focused on her plate again. She liked Curt. He was a laid-back guy who had gotten into the insurance business on the recommendation of his wife some thirty years before. Sharlene was the driving force behind the company, and since she kept the books, she knew when to prod her husband along. She was also the person that had turned down a raise for Lauren for the fifth time just the week before.

If it wasn't for Cory, Lauren probably would have left the company years ago, since all the claims they'd made upon hiring her had yet to be fulfilled. Paid vacations, something she'd done once or twice, never turned out to be paid. Quarterly raises had turned into just moving her up periodically when the minimum wage had to be raised. "It's a family business," they would often say. "We all win, and we all lose together."

Shaking off the thoughts, Lauren tried to listen in to some of the conversations going on around the table. It seemed that with the start of each one, the formers raised their voices louder and louder, making it difficult to decipher anything.

Dinner finished sometime later, and Lauren filled up the sink, ready to help with the dishes.

"What are you doing, Lauren?" Sharlene asked, bringing her plate into the kitchen.

"I just thought I'd help with the dishes. Thank you so much for dinner." She paused a second, willing the half-truth to slide from her lips. "It was great."

Sharlene's eyes narrowed, and Lauren wasn't sure whether she was in trouble or if she'd somehow frozen the woman in place. "Okay, well, thank you." She set her plate down on a stack of other plates and left the room.

Lauren bit her upper lip, glancing around the kitchen. Not one of the Turner family was anywhere in sight. Turning back to the sink, she shut off the water and picked up the scrubber from the side of the faucet. She'd gotten herself into this mess; she may as well do something to win over her co-boss and boyfriend's mother.

* * *

IT TOOK over an hour to get all the dishes loaded in the dishwasher and the large pots and pans scrubbed, but Lauren felt accomplished once she'd finished. After wiping her hands on a towel, she stepped out of the room, looking for Cory. She wasn't sure what his family normally did on holidays, but she would be the supportive girlfriend.

There was no sign of him in the family room with his father and sisters, so she wandered around, glancing at some of the pieces of art on the walls. They were quite striking, and she wasn't sure how long she'd been staring at one until she heard voices in the hall just down from her.

"When are you going to move on?" Sharlene, of course.

"When I find the one I'll spend forever with. For now, I'm good just coasting along." Cory sounded like he was talking about what he wanted for breakfast, not a real care in the world.

Lauren felt as though the bar on her brothers' set of weights was resting against her chest, pushing down with every second and making it hard to breathe.

"I have a couple of girls I can set you up with. You're my only boy and deserve so much better than someone who makes minimum wage."

Anger seeped through Lauren's body and into her face. She'd heard enough to last her a lifetime of embarrassment. The frustration that had built up since telling Cody about the pie was ready to explode, and all sense of propriety fled as she marched down the hall. Once she turned the corner to face the two of them, their eyes wide with guilt caused her to pause a moment.

"I'll help you with that, Sharlene. The only reason I've stayed with your company and gone without a raise since the day I started working for you all, which isn't what you promised at the beginning and I'm pretty sure could be taken to court over, is because of your son here. I thought I loved hım enough to be his wife, but it seems I dodged a bullet." She turned to face Cory, whose face was as white as a sheet. "We're done. And I quit. Good luck actually doing your job for once."

She looked between the two of them, both of their normal smugness wiped from their faces. Lauren stalked down the hall to grab her coat and purse before they could respond and then turned to walk outside as she looked up the number to a taxi service. As she left, her eyes caught on the shocked expressions of the rest of the family as they were turned in her direction.

So what if she'd been turned into some sideshow. She was done with this waiting, this hoping that her life would change. She'd just have to make a change herself and stop waiting for the world to do it for her.

CHAPTER 5

*A*fter securing a cab a block or two away from the Turner home, she watched the scenery pass, trying to decide what to do with her life. She'd just broken up with her boyfriend and quit her job, all within two sentences. What else was keeping her in Fort Collins?

The ache of homesickness was overwhelming, and she took out her phone, the tears falling freely now. After dialing her dad's number, she waited for it to ring a few times and was surprised when he picked up the phone.

"Lauren, dear. Happy Thanksgiving."

"You too, Dad." She sniffled, hoping he hadn't heard it.

"What's wrong? Is everything okay? You're not hurt, are you?" The protective tone of her father's voice caused her to smile, and for the first time in several years, she knew the only place she wanted to be was back home in Coldwater Creek.

Lauren bit the side of her tongue, focusing on the pain so she didn't cry even more. "Cory and I broke up, and I quit my job. I'm in a cab right now on my way back to my apartment. Can I come stay for the weekend?" Her voice raised in pitch toward the end, the impact of what happened minutes before hitting her like a load of bricks.

"You can stay for a lot longer than that if you need." He paused, and she could hear his breath coming through the phone. "I've missed you, girl."

"I've missed you too, Daddy. I'm so sorry it's been so long. But you know how it—"

"Yes," he said, cutting her off. "I know how hard it was for you. But I'll take whatever time I can get with my girl. With all of your brothers around the house, they could use a special dose of your mothering right now." His chuckle sent the homesickness straight to her heart. She was the second child and the only daughter with four brothers. Her mother used to say she knew how to nag from the moment she could talk.

Smiling at the small memory, Lauren realized she hadn't been that fiery person she'd always been, not in the time she'd dated Cory. He'd been her first real boyfriend, and as the cab pulled up to her townhouse, she realized she'd been doing everything she thought Cory would like just so he wouldn't break up with her. What a waste of three and a half good years of her life.

Reflecting on all the little jabs and cut-downs from Cory over the years, she realized she'd never really been in love with him, just the idea that someone called her their girl-friend. Grinding her teeth together, she decided she'd never let the opinions of a guy change her personality; otherwise, she'd just be wasting her time yet again. She wouldn't settle again.

"I'll throw some clothes into a bag and head out, probably around three or so."

"Remember to drive slow if there is snow and spend the night somewhere. I don't want you driving all that way when it gets dark." It was her father's voice, but it reminded her so much of her mother that her throat tightened.

Lauren closed her eyes, breathing slowly, and smiled. "I'll be careful." Her tone sounded more like a teenager than a twenty-five-year-old adult.

"A father never stops worrying about his children, Lauren. Just remember that."

They said goodbye, and her father's last words ran on a loop through her head. She was grateful to have such a loving family, even if she was the only daughter.

She now had no idea what she wanted to do with her life, and the thought was frightening as she threw winter clothes into a large suitcase. But that was something that time at the farm could help her figure out. At least, she hoped.

By 3:15, Lauren had packed a few bags into her Honda Civic, the one she'd bought secondhand in high school that had made it through college and the last several years. It was getting older, but she'd needed the money from her job to have a roof over her head and food to eat. She didn't mind that it was older, and she'd worked to take good care of it. She just hoped it could make the eight-hour trek back to Coldwater Creek.

Closer to nine that night, she tried to figure out what to do. The urge to get home made her want to continue on, and the caffeinated drinks she'd picked up when she had to refuel would keep her awake for the last two hours. But the roads were the most winding and snow-packed as she got closer to her hometown, and the snow had begun to fall.

She could hear the snow flipping up against the sides of her car, and every once in a while, she slid an inch or two, keeping her vigilant in having her eyes on the road.

Passing the last chance to stay the night, Lauren forged ahead, leaning forward so she could see beyond the snowflakes and the swooshing of her wipers. The lights were sparse in this part of Wyoming, and even though she knew the road like the back of her hand, there was still a small knot forming in her stomach, causing her to tighten her hands on the wheel. Both sides of the roads had walls of plowed snow, and the wind was whipping it slowly back across the highway.

At one point, she was at a near crawl, finally passing an accident on a two-lane road. She was so close now. She smiled as she passed through the town of Afton, knowing she was just that much closer to the comfort of her family home.

The car in front of her turned off the road, leaving it open. The anxious feeling took over again as the snow was getting thicker at an alarming rate, but she just needed to see the lights in her house, the beautiful log home her father had painstakingly kept stained over the years.

Her phone sounded, and she glanced down for a second. As she faced forward again, a large deer stood in her path. She slammed on the brakes, causing the car to fishtail on the slick road. Trying to correct, she turned the wheel to the left, but her foot slipped, sending the car careening forward as she pushed the gas pedal.

Why hadn't she stopped when she should have? Her windshield cleared, and her lights shone on just how much snow was on the road. What had she been thinking?

By the time she freed her foot, she barely had time to hit the brake before the front of her car hit a log gate. As the airbag deployed, her head smacked against it, and blackness enveloped her.

CHAPTER 6

Walker jumped out of bed and opened the curtains, wondering what the sound had been that had jarred him awake. He couldn't see anything clearly because of the tree line just outside the lodge, but there were lights shining down there.

"Come on, Bear. Let's go see what happened." After pulling on jeans and a long-sleeved shirt, he walked down to the mudroom to slip on his snow boots and thick winter coat. Once the door opened, Bear ran outside, straight in the direction of the lights. Walker jogged to keep up with him, feeling the sleep disappear against the cold Wyoming night.

By the time they made it to the main gate and around the fence, Walker saw a car lodged into his fence. He picked up speed, knowing that if he could do anything to help the driver, he had to act now.

As he knocked on the window, he saw the silhouette of someone hunched over the steering wheel. The sound wasn't phasing whoever it was. He worked to open the door, prying it apart as a section of it had been crushed with the impact.

"Ma'am, can you hear me?" he asked, seeing long hair. "You just crashed into the fence. Are you okay?"

Again, no response. He was glad he'd thought to grab his phone and pulled it out, dialing his friend down at the fire department.

"Walker, what are you doing up this late?" Ethan Montgomery asked, sounding like he'd been awake for hours.

"A car just crashed into the fence in front of the lodge. I need the ambulance to come out."

"I'm sorry, Walk. They just shut the roads down about fifteen minutes ago, and our snowcat is taking care of another accident up the canyon. With the snow and wind blowing, the drifts are filling in the roads quickly. We can't leave Afton. I'm surprised a car got that far past town. I'll call you when they get back, and we'll head your way."

Panic surged through him. What was he supposed to do for this girl? He only had basic training for first aid, mostly to sew up cuts he'd gotten after a rough bull ride.

"Can you talk me through this, then? She's hunched forward on the airbag."

Walker pinched the phone between his cheek and neck, checking vitals as Ethan walked him through the process. The girl's legs and arms all responded to stimuli, reassuring Walker that she wasn't paralyzed.

"Am I okay to move her?"

"I would. They say the temperature is going to drop to below zero tonight, and the storm is just beginning. Be careful and call me if you have any problems."

Walker thanked him before hanging up. He stuck the phone into his pocket and leaned forward, wrapping one arm around the girl's back and the other under her knees, pulling her out of the car. Bear let out a loud howl, which caused the girl to stir, but her eyes never opened, at least from what Walker could see in the near pitch-dark of the night.

He made his way through the high snow, fighting against the wind that had picked up. It would be quite some time now for anyone to get through, as the wind was fierce, causing the snowdrifts to shift into the road, making it difficult to see where the ditches lay on either side.

Once inside the warm lodge, he noticed the fire had gone out, but at least it wasn't as cold as outside right then. Walker placed the girl on the couch, adjusting a pillow under her head and pulling a blanket over her legs. He turned on a small light on a side table and turned back to her, gasping as the light shone on her face. Lauren Burke.

It had been a few years since he'd seen her, probably not since her mother's funeral, but it was definitely her. A cut sliced across the side of her forehead, the blood still a bright red. He walked to the closet and retrieved several clean cloths and his first aid kit.

He cleaned the wound as best as he could and watched her stiffen a moment as the antiseptic took effect. She still didn't open her eyes, and Walker was glad he knew exactly what to do in this kind of situation. With four of his siblings being part of the rodeo circuit, there had been many occasions when he'd have to patch up one or more of them.

Once he'd cleaned the slice, he realized it could be closed with butterfly strips, which would leave minimal scarring. Not that the Lauren he'd known had been overly into looks, but lying there in front of him, she was beautiful, and he didn't want her to be marred with any missed stitches.

When he opened the box of strips, the sound must have woken her because her eyes opened wide and she sat up, her eyes darting around the room.

"Where am I? Who are you? How did I get here?" Her eyes

focused on his face, and a few seconds later, she relaxed. "Walker?"

"That would be me. How are you feeling?" Walker asked.

"A little confused," she said, moving her hand to rub at her forehead.

Walker stopped her hand from hitting the wound, and a strange feeling of excitement pulsed through him as he stared at their hands.

He lowered her hand slowly and pointed to her forehead. "You got a cut. I was just trying to fix it."

"How did I get cut? And you didn't tell me where I am." Her eyes widened as she looked around the room.

"This is the Silver Brook Lodge. I—"

"Walker, I'm not crazy. The lodge burned down when we were really young. How can this be it?"

Walker tried to hold back a grin, knowing it had been a while since she'd been home. She was cute when she was defiant like that.

He shook his head. "I had it rebuilt over the last year." He glanced back to her cut, which was now oozing a little more because of her movements. "You crashed into my fence a little bit ago. Just let me get this patched up, and you'll be good to go. I'm just glad you didn't have any extensive injuries. We'd both probably still be out in the dark, freezing to death."

After the last few words, it was as if something clicked in her brain. "Crashed into your fence? I remember there was a deer and I swerved to miss it, but with the slush on the road, my old tires didn't quite make it."

"Can I ask why you were driving so late at night anyway? My friend in Afton said they closed the roads just a few minutes after you must have gone through."

Lauren looked down at her hands, biting her bottom lip. "I should have gotten a hotel somewhere. I didn't leave Fort

Collins until three this afternoon, but I was just so anxious to get home that I decided to risk it. Do you have a truck or something that can take me to my dad's?"

Walker wasn't sure how to say it, but if things were closed in town, it would be hard for a snowplow to make it through there within the next twenty-four hours.

"I have a truck, but I don't think it will make it through all the snow outside. It's turned into a blizzard outside, and even though the farm is a few miles away, we wouldn't make it through without incident. I have guest rooms you can stay in tonight, and we can reevaluate tomorrow. Does that work for you?" He kept his expression neutral, knowing she didn't really have another choice, unless she wanted to start walking down the road in the knee-high snowdrifts. With the uptick in amount of snow falling and the wind that seemed to only increase in howling, he just hoped she'd take him up on his offer.

"That can work."

Walker watched as her eyes shifted around the room, taking in the log structure he'd worked so hard to get finished. Part of him hoped she'd approve of it, bringing back the memory of the old building to Coldwater Creek.

"Hold still. I'm just going to butterfly the cut together so it can start to heal." He scooted closer to her, inhaling the apple cinnamon smell about her. It reminded him of Christmas and traditions, causing him to smile slightly. He pulled out the strips and focused on the cut, knowing her eyes were staring at his face the entire time.

After placing the strips over the wound, he sat back. "That should do it, for tonight at least. Let me show you to your room. Are you okay to walk?"

Lauren's face showed a mixture of emotions, but they passed so fast that Walker couldn't decipher them. "I should be fine." She reached her hand up for him, and he helped her stand, that same electricity flowing through them. What was that about?

She'd always been the annoying younger sister of Preston, the one who'd follow them around like a puppy just to see what they were doing. She'd definitely grown up in the years since, and Walker found himself pulled to her with an invisible tether. Were these feelings just a rebound of Cara ditching him for Roper Grand? That had been over a year ago and more of a blessing than he could see at the time. No, this was something else.

He showed her to the first guest room on the second floor, making sure the light worked and that the bed had been made.

"Uh, do you have something to change into?" he asked, looking down at her jeans and sweater.

With a shy smile, Lauren said, "Yes, but it's out in my car." She paused a moment before saying, "I should be good with these. I can go get my bags in the morning."

Walker nodded, moving away from the door. As he walked down the stairs, he realized he was still in his warm clothes and boots. Now was as good a time as any to go grab her bags. He hated sleeping in jeans himself and didn't want her to be uncomfortable staying there. She was the unofficial first guest of the lodge, and he wanted to make sure it was a good experience.

Checking his phone before he walked outside, he saw he'd missed a call from the Afton fire department, probably checking in to see how things had gone. He'd gotten a text from Ethan saying the plows were working on the roads to get to them but it would still be several hours before they could tow Lauren's car to a shop.

It was a good thing he was getting Lauren's belongings now.

"Let's go, Bear. One more trip outside."

Bear wagged his tail as he waited for Walker to open the door. He darted outside again, sniffing the ground in the deepening snow. Walker had never seen it this bad before. This part of Wyoming was known for getting a lot of snow, but in one storm, this was more than he could remember in his twenty-eight years of life.

Lauren was lucky she'd made it through her accident with only a gash to the head. And for some strange reason, Walker was more grateful for that than anything else.

CHAPTER 7

*L*auren watched Walker as he walked down the hall toward the stairs. She didn't think it was possible to get any more attractive than he'd been when she was a senior in high school. But with his broad shoulders and a scar along his jaw, she had to work to keep her own jaw from dropping each time he looked at her.

She'd had a crush on him since she was young, probably when she first met him. And he'd always thought of her as the annoying little sister, well, as far as Preston expressed. Walker had never been one to use more words than necessary, and the tender way he'd taken care of her tonight had made her insides do somersaults over and over.

What were the odds that she'd leave probably the worst boyfriend in the world only to wind up being rescued by the man of her dreams?

Shaking her head, she tried to rid herself of those thoughts. It wasn't likely that his feelings went any deeper than they had years ago before she'd left for Colorado. But with the way he looked and the smell of pine from his cologne, the old feelings of a crush came rushing back to her.

Taking a seat on the bed, she wasn't sure what to do. She wasn't really tired now as the shock of her accident sank in and she relived it over again. He'd had to carry her in, which set off a swarm of butterflies in her stomach.

A knock came at the door a few minutes later, causing her to jump. She stood and wondered what she could have forgotten. When she opened the door, Walker stood there again, his cheeks pink and his dark hair tousled, making him look even better than before.

"Yes?" she said, trying to focus.

"I figured you'd be more comfortable in a change of clothes. It's hard for me to sleep if I haven't brushed my teeth, so I thought I'd run out and get your things for you. Let me know if you need anything. I, uh, I'm in the bedroom on the first floor past the kitchen." He gave her a small smile and turned, motioning for his dog to follow him.

"Thank you. You didn't have to do this." As she stared into his face, adoration overwhelmed her. Cory would never have done something so selfless as trudge through thick snow if it didn't benefit him in some way.

Walker turned back to her and smiled. "It's nothing. Just call me the bellboy." He nodded and disappeared down the hallway. He walked with a slight limp, and she wondered what had caused it. But then her brain registered the way his jeans cut just right, and she knew she was in trouble.

The feelings churning through her were a thousand times stronger than anything she'd ever felt for Cory Turner, but was that just the effect of breaking up with her boyfriend of three and a half years several hours before? She was going to have to keep her feelings in check and make it through until tomorrow. Hopefully, the roads would be cleared by then so she could get home and figure out how to salvage her life from the mess it was in.

She crossed into her bathroom and pulled out her toothbrush and toothpaste, smiling as she thought of Walker's comment. How a famous bull rider could still be so quiet was beyond her. She'd attended plenty of big rodeos during her life, as Preston had competed as a bronc rider, but she'd known that most of the bull riders were arrogant and self-centered.

But not Walker. He somehow took the credit and spread it out amongst his team of trainers and family. It didn't seem like much had changed on that front, and it made her smile even wider, knowing there was at least one decent man left in the world.

She took in the trim work of the bathroom and recalled the great room. What would cause Walker to build a lodge when the National Rodeo Finals were coming up in about a week?

The house was quiet and dark as she made her way to the bed. She wished she could call her father at this hour to let him know she was okay. It would also be nice to get all the details of Coldwater Creek since her mother had passed. Walker's sister, Kassidy, would be ideal, but it was already past midnight, and she hadn't been very good at keeping in touch with her old best friend in the first place.

Coldwater Creek was already different than she remembered it, but part of that was her problem for staying away for so long. She just hoped she'd get some sign of what she was supposed to do with her life. She could really use a Christmas miracle.

CHAPTER 8

*B*ear woke Walker earlier than he wanted, just before six in the morning. He readjusted and closed his eyes again, feeling exhausted from some strange dream from the night before. Another nudge in the side caused Walker to sit up, knowing he wasn't going to get much more sleep.

He pulled his jeans on from the side of the bed and moved to the back door, letting Bear out to relieve himself. The sun in the sky still hadn't broken the horizon, but the light gray clouds above seemed to brighten the mounds of snow outside the door. They were at least up to his thigh with thick flakes still floating to the ground. This was one of the times he was grateful he didn't live at home anymore. He'd have had to trudge out and feed all the animals no matter the weather or the day.

There wasn't a way he'd be able to dig his way out completely today, but he'd have to try; otherwise, the snow would just keep accumulating. After pulling on his snow boots and coat, he looked for his gloves and hat under the mound of clothes he'd been meaning to wash.

By the time he got to the small shed just twenty yards from the back of the lodge, he was breathing heavier than normal, the movement through the snow feeling like one of those training regiments his father used to make him do when he was still bull riding. He pulled out a shovel and started on the walk, feeling the weight of the wet snow after only a few shovelfuls.

A memory popped into his mind, and he chuckled. One of the guys he used to compete with didn't believe there were two types of snow, having grown up in the South. When Walker had tried to explain that sometimes there was a light, fluffy snow and others a wet, heavy snow, the guy had given him a look like Walker had ten heads.

He worked quickly, clearing the sidewalk in several minutes. Bear jumped around in the snow, rolling in it and flipping it up into the air, causing some small piles to fall back onto the cleaned sidewalk. Walker smiled at him before looking in the direction of his truck on the other end of the property where he always parked it. It was going to take hours to get a trail dug for him to get out, but after a quick glance at the road, it didn't look like a plow had made it through yet.

A sliver of silver caught his eye, and the events from the night before came flooding back, not a dream after all. Lauren's car still sat in front of the fence, stuck with everything else in this part of the Coldwater Creek Valley.

Taking a break, he went back inside, Bear at his heels. Walker took off his snow clothes, wondering what he would make for breakfast. Did Lauren even eat breakfast? Or was she one of those strictly cereal people? He'd never known her that intimately, and the thought that he'd have to talk to her for longer than last night sent a chill through him, excitement mixed with terror.

He thought back to the connection when he touched her

skin and wondered if she'd felt it too. It had been so long since he'd even thought about another girl that he wanted to run back to his room and hide out until she found a way home. But he could hear his mother's voice in his head, telling him that wasn't how one treated guests. And if the lodge was going to work out in the long run, he'd have to get used to the hospitality and customer service parts of the business, something that now freaked him out the closer it came to opening day.

Sighing, he walked into the kitchen and opened the fridge. It was well-stocked with food, which was now a blessing since he wasn't sure when they would be able to get to a store. After pulling out a carton of eggs and a package of bacon, he turned on the gas to the stove and put a pan on top.

With the bacon sizzling and the eggs cooking on the griddle in the middle of the stove, Walker turned to stir the frozen orange juice in a large pitcher. He was grateful for his mother and sisters and all they'd done to set up this kitchen with the necessary tools the future chef would need. And that he'd paid attention to pick up a few cooking skills from his mother. He was no chef by any means, but he didn't starve.

"Wow, do you do this every morning?" a voice asked from behind him.

Walker turned and grinned at Lauren, whose hair fell in waves around her face. She looked beautiful, even just having woken up, and he wondered if she'd always looked like that. The pink in her cheeks reminded him of when they were younger. She always seemed to have rosy cheeks when she was around. The thought of simpler days made him smile wider.

"Not every morning, but it helps to eat something other than cold cereal when there's a lot to be done around the place." He gestured to a chair on the other side of the island. "Take a seat. How do you like your eggs?"

"Scrambled, if you don't mind. That bacon smells delicious." She took a seat, her eyes wide.

"Chewy or crispy?" Walker asked, turning the bacon over.

"Crispy."

He turned to smile at her and said, "Me too. Juice? Milk?"

"Wow, I feel like this is some kind of twenty questions for breakfast," Lauren said, tipping her head back and laughing. The sound reverberated through Walker's chest, and he laughed too. "Juice, definitely juice."

After plating and pouring, Walker set the meal in front of her. He turned to do the same for his own meal and took it around the large island to sit next to her.

"Thank you for this. I haven't had a home-cooked breakfast since, well, it's been a while."

"Lots of cold cereal?" Walker asked with a smirk.

Lauren twisted her lips to the side as if she were embarrassed to answer. "Lots of cold cereal. I'm impressed you even know how to cook this well. My boyfriend—I mean ex-boyfriend—didn't know how to cook toast, let alone eggs and bacon."

Walker nodded, taking a sip of his juice. So, she'd had a boyfriend, and it sounded fairly recent. What had gone wrong in their relationship? That was a sign to him to back off and put the reins on the feelings that seemed to surge every time she was in the room.

He hadn't recognized the feelings from when they were younger, but she'd always been a great listener growing up. For those random times when he'd had to make major life decisions, she'd always been the one to listen to his fears and help him put things into perspective. That realization made him smile, surprised he'd never identified it before.

"I've been meaning to ask you, what are you doing with

the lodge?" she asked. "I mean, aren't you busy getting ready for the rodeo finals?" She took a bite of her eggs and turned her gaze back on him.

Walker shuddered, memories of his injury flashing through his mind in a split-second. "I, uh, I got hurt last year. After surgeries and several scans, I decided it was best to hang up the spurs and find something else to do with my life." He focused on his plate, not wanting to see the disappointment or incredulity he'd usually see in people's faces. He'd been in the top three in the world for nearly five years, so for him to give up bull riding had been a shock for most.

He turned his head when Lauren set her hand on his arm. "I'm sorry. It must have been hard to give up something you've loved your whole life and then try to figure out what to do with yourself after. Do you have any lingering pains or injuries?"

"I have aches and pains, but that's understandable since I've done bull riding since I was young."

"Are you going to the finals this year? Your brothers and sisters are all still in it, right?"

Walker gave her a half-smile and nodded. "The last time I talked to Kassidy, she said this might be her last year. I haven't decided yet whether I'll go or not. Opening day for the lodge and the hotel is in less than two weeks, and there's still a lot to accomplish. I just hope there's enough time for the rest of the materials to come in with all this snow."

Lauren gasped as she looked out the window. "It's still snowing? How high is it now?"

"It was about mid-waist when I went out earlier. It doesn't look like the snowplow has been by either. You might be here an extra day." He grimaced, not sure how she'd take that news.

She glanced around, and her shoulders visibly relaxed. "Anywhere is better than Fort Collins right now. And this place is really nice, so I can't complain. Besides, the service is amazing." She lifted her juice and winked at him, sending that trickle of excitement flowing through him.

"That's my first review, so I'll take it. I have a bunch of little things around the lodge to do today, but if you need me, just let me know." He took his plate to the sink and rinsed it out, leaving it in the dish drainer. He hated using the dishwasher when it was just him and Bear.

"Thank you. I need to call my dad and let him know I'm all right. He'll give me an earful when he hears that I tried to drive through the storm, but I'm glad you saved me." She gave him a look that was a mixture of pleased and embarrassed. "After that, I'll probably just be online, looking for jobs. I need to at least figure out a part of my life before I head back to Colorado."

Walker wanted to pry, but he didn't want to make her feel uncomfortable, so he just said, "There are always jobs around Coldwater Creek."

She nodded as though she hadn't thought of that until he'd said something. "That's true. I'll have to look around." She followed what he'd done by rinsing her plate and wiped her hands on her ice cream flannel pajama pants. "Thank you again for breakfast. It was perfect."

Walker waved to her as she wandered out of the room. As much as he kept telling himself to keep his distance for the limited amount of time they'd be together, the other part of him wanted to hug her to him and solve all her problems for her.

He'd always had a soft spot for quietly solving people's problems, maybe because it distracted him from his own. When he'd realized Cara had broken up with him, he'd found Bear at a rescue the same day. The center had claimed he wasn't adoptable after the abuse he'd suffered, but after a little work, he'd become the best dog Walker could have asked for.

He knew he couldn't fix everyone's problems that easily, but the pull toward Lauren made him itch to help her. Not to mention the comfort he felt around her, and when she smiled, he may as well be a puddle on the floor.

CHAPTER 9

*L*auren rubbed at her eyes. It was well past noon, and she'd been staring at her laptop since breakfast. Breakfast…every time she thought about it, she wondered what she'd ever seen in Cory. He never would have done something so kind as to make or do anything for her without an ulterior motive.

She'd called her father, and while she'd been right about his frustration in putting herself in danger, he sounded glad she was safe.

Once they ended their call, she'd dived into her job search, and after going through all the classifieds and different businesses in Fort Collins and surrounding areas, she'd moved her focus to Coldwater Creek, wondering if Walker was right about the availability of jobs.

There were more than she'd thought, but not many of them were what she was looking for. She wasn't desperate for any job just yet, but she knew that time would come if she didn't find something soon.

After taking a quick shower, she changed into some fleece-lined leggings and a large sweater and pulled her wet hair into a quick bun. Just doing that helped her feel a little better.

She reminded herself that she'd been through a lot in the past few years while working at the Turner family company. As she walked down the stairs, she ticked off the responsibilities she'd been given in those three and a half years: customer service, management of other employees, payroll. She'd also rearranged and organized the entire office once when the family had gone on a cruise. With all of those skills, surely her future wouldn't be a complete failure.

Not that she was ever complimented or compensated for the work she did above her job responsibilities for them—which now, in hindsight, made her burn with frustration. How any company could thrive when they treated their employees like second-rate citizens was beyond her. As she thought of her relationship with Cory over the past years, she knew, just as she'd told Sharlene, she'd dodged a bullet. She just wished she'd been able to see it all sooner.

A fire was going in the wood-burning stove in the large gathering room, and Walker's dog was curled up on the rug in front of it, taking a nap. This whole scene was so different than everything she'd seen over the past few years, and it made her homesick, even though she was only a few miles from home at the moment.

She sighed, and a sound from the kitchen caused her to jump. Walker came into view and must have seen her startled face because he extended both arms, hands out as if talking her down from panic.

"Sorry, I just heard you and wanted to make sure you were okay. Can I make you some lunch or get you something to drink?"

Lauren gave him a half-smile, seeing the sincerity in his eyes. "You're on your way to working in hospitality. That's a good thing."

His cheeks colored, and he stuffed his hands into his pockets, shifting nervously. He was adorable when he was embarrassed. "I can only hope. There are times when I wonder what I was thinking, taking over something like this. How to ride bulls, I know. Managing and hiring people, or even making a simple spreadsheet…now, that's all over my head." His shoulders sagged as though he'd been kicked in the gut and wasn't sure how to attack once standing.

"See, now, spreadsheets are something I can't live without. Do you mind if I take a look and help you with it?" She took a few steps forward.

Walker took a step back, allowing her to pass to the table where the laptop sat. "I'd appreciate that. It's one of those things that never clicked in school."

Lauren sat in the chair next to the computer and pulled it toward her, letting her eyes scan the screen to get the gist of what he was trying to organize. "Is this a spreadsheet for income and expenses?"

Walker nodded, sitting in the seat next to her and rubbing his chin. "That's what I want it to be. Right now, it's just looking like a bunch of random numbers in columns."

As Lauren looked at the list of descriptions, she knew the easiest way to make life simpler for Walker later was to create different groupings. After adding another column, she turned and caught the look of horror on his face.

She placed a hand on his arm, hoping to reassure him she was, in fact, helping. But the result of the shock from the touch caused her brain to blank for several seconds, and her eyes drifted to his lips, the thought about how soft they looked crossing her mind.

"I promise this will make things easier later. Let's put these into categories so if you need to know how much you're spending in an area, you can just quickly sort it." She clicked on the top box and moved the cursor down slowly so she could highlight the sort function. "After we come up with your categories, we can work on setting up the sums and totals of the different columns. As long as you don't delete the formula, you should have accurate numbers from there." She gave him a small smile, and he nodded, looking as though he was still processing everything she'd said.

She'd known Walker for years, and he was by no means dumb, but she could understand how hard it would be to figure out this kind of stuff when he hadn't ever done it before.

Filling in descriptions took about ten minutes of brainstorming before they settled on the names of each category he'd need for the business. Then she helped Walker with the formulas needed to total each of the columns.

"Okay, so now we have it split into office supplies and amenities—the little complimentary soaps and stuff you'll include in each room. Here you can include what you've spent on furniture and décor." She scrolled down a bit and was about to keep explaining, when he spoke up.

"I think I've got all that. I just put the expense in this column, and then anything I make goes into the income column, correct?"

Lauren nodded, grinning at him. "Yes. If you keep an accurate account of everything, maybe checking at the end of the day, your taxes will be so much easier to figure out at the end of the year." She turned back to the computer.

She could feel the heat of Walker's gaze on her face, and she pretended to focus on the screen for as long as she could before the pull caused her to turn in his direction. His features were soft, and they were so close that goosebumps popped up along her arms. She rubbed at them, which broke Walker's gaze.

"Are you cold? We can go closer to the fire." He picked up the laptop and waited for her to stand and walk in front of him. It wasn't until she sat on the couch that she realized they'd be sitting that much closer than they were in the chairs at the table.

He sat next to her, placing the laptop across their legs. That smell of pine filled her nose again and heightened all her senses, making her hyperaware of his leg barely touching hers.

Why she'd never experienced anything like this around Cory, she had no idea. Was it because she'd always had a crush on Walker that things seemed to be exaggerated? Her defenses against her attraction for him were weakening, and she would need to finish this up as soon as she could to give them some space. Otherwise, she might end up with a real broken heart.

They worked on filling out everything he could remember, and she pushed the laptop back to him. She hadn't felt this good about finishing a project since she'd pitched the idea to help with the Medicare applications at Turner Insurance several months ago. That had taken some convincing, but for once, Carl had stood up to his wife's rantings and overruled her.

"How do you feel about that? Do you need any other spreadsheets created?" Lauren asked Walker, seeing the hint of a smile around his lips. It was strange staring at him after all those years of secretly crushing on him, seeing a more vulnerable side than the strong, silent type he'd always exuded.

"That helps me quite a bit, thank you. I think you just taught me something in fifteen minutes that I didn't learn throughout one semester of my computer class." Walker leaned back and grinned, brushing a hand through his hair as his eyes stayed locked on the computer screen. He finally turned to her and asked, "How did you learn how to do all this? I thought Preston said you were an art major or some-thing like that."

Lauren chuckled, pulling her feet onto the couch and wrapping her arms around her knees. She was beaming at the compliment he'd paid her and couldn't seem to tamp down the feeling. "Art History, actually. And no, I didn't learn how to do this in college. I've been working at an insurance company for the past few years and had to learn quickly how to keep information organized. My favorite thing to do has always been to organize, so I think that helped a bit."

Walker nodded with a close-lipped smile. "Are there not a lot of jobs in art history?"

"There are a few," she said, a little flood of shame running through her chest. She looked down, picking at her finger-nails. "It wasn't until I graduated that I realized getting a job in that field meant more school or an amazing streak of luck to get a good internship. I didn't have more money to go on and had started dating someone. His parents owned an insurance company, and they offered me a job, so I've worked there for the last three and a half years."

"I take it you didn't completely enjoy it?" Walker asked, one eyebrow rising in emphasis to the question.

Lauren let out a loud laugh, one of those awkward kinds that came sailing out and was louder than she meant. "I'm sorry, um, that's just a loaded question. If you'd asked me a week ago, I would have said I was helping out the family I thought I would eventually be a part of."

A few seconds of silence ticked by as she tried to decipher her thoughts and feelings, working to put them into align-ment. He shifted as he took in the news, and she wondered what he was thinking.

"And? What happened?" Walker finally asked, moving his arm to the top of the couch behind her. She knew it wasn't supposed to be a romantic gesture, only a way to turn and see her better, but her stomach still reacted as though at any moment he would lean over and kiss her with those perfect lips.

Lauren groaned. "Thanksgiving happened. The first time he'd invited me to a family holiday in all the time we'd dated. It was more of a train wreck than I'd ever imagined, but it seemed like everything came into focus all in a matter of two hours, or however long I was at their house."

She covered her face with her hands and dragged them down her cheeks, embarrassed to continue. "You know, I never got a pay raise in all the years I was there? And most of the time, I had to cover for Cory in meetings with clients because he was the only boy in the family and his mother treated him like he was the most amazing gift to the world, never caring if he was showing up and doing his job or not." Shaking her head, Lauren still couldn't believe she'd survived that long under the guise that she would eventually be married.

Walker narrowed his eyes as he studied her face, and Lauren shifted, feeling uncomfortable at such a look. "So, what made Cory so great in the beginning? There had to be reasons why you liked him and continued dating for that amount of time, right?"

Lauren tapped her pointer finger against her lips, trying to figure out the best answer to Walker's question. She'd had over eight hours to ponder on that exact question, but the truth made her sound like some dumb girl swept up over the idea of love.

"Honestly, I think he was the first guy to show interest in me. He was my first boyfriend—"

"Really? You, Lauren Burke, have only had one boyfriend in your life?" The disbelief on his face caused Lauren to pause.

Blinking a few times, she finally said, "What does that

mean?" She could hear the edge to her voice and took a breath, curious as to his answer.

"Look, the Lauren I remember always had a bunch of guys following her around in high school. You never dated them?"

"I dated a few of them, yes. But never to the status of boyfriend/girlfriend. I always wondered if there was some magical aspect that led from one date or a couple of dates to 'we're exclusive.'"

"You are also the only girl in your family with four brothers. I bet the element of intimidation had something to do with guys not getting too close." Walker chuckled, the wry smile making Lauren realize the truth of his words.

Her mouth dropped open as she processed it for several moments. "Preston."

Walker nodded, and a small amount of betrayal from her older brother twisted her stomach. She'd have to have a talk with him.

"Well, Cory just started calling me his girlfriend after our second date, and as surprised as I was, I was also flattered." Biting her bottom lip for a few seconds, she looked up at Walker, a mischievous smile on her face. "What about your relationships, Mr. McBride?"

He grimaced and shook his head. "That makes me sound like my father. Let's stick with Walker." He laughed a minute before his face sobered. "I've only had one girlfriend as well, but that was by choice."

"I know that's not a lie. There were plenty of young women tripping over themselves trying to snag you in high school." She liked seeing him squirm, and her comments did just that.

"I was so focused on riding and rodeo that anything that wasn't a horse or a bull didn't matter much to me. We were always training so much, always on the road during the summer, that even the thought of a relationship was laughable." He paused, his eyes glazed over as if reliving memories.

Lauren's curiosity got the best of her, and she finally asked, "So, what was it about this one girlfriend that made you change your mind?"

"She was the sister of one of my competitors, and she seemed pretty chill and down-to-earth at first. Persistence was definitely one of her talents because she would always corner me and talk to me about how great a couple we'd make, and she knew a lot about bull riding. We started dating, and I was surprised by how nice it was to have someone in the crowd other than my family cheering me on."

After an intake of breath, he stood, pacing before the fireplace. "We dated about two years, mostly just seeing each other at each rodeo event and texting or calling a lot in between. I'd bought a ring, thinking two years was a long time to date someone I cared about. Then I got hurt."

Lauren said nothing, knowing he had to be going through everything that happened with an injury like that. She wished her family had told her about it so she could have sent him a card or something.

"Things seemed to change so fast that I wasn't quite sure what was happening until the aftermath. She was there for the first few appointments, but when the talk turned to the fact that I might never ride again, I saw less and less of her. Turns out, she liked the attention that came with being my girlfriend, and if I wasn't going back to the arena, she wasn't going to give that up. She ended up with another bull rider, Roper Grand." Agony was etched into Walker's face.

Lauren stood and, on impulse, walked over and slid her arms around him, giving him a hug that she was surprised to find she needed just as much. "I'm so sorry, Walk. It looks like it's a blessing we didn't end up with who we were dating." She held on for a few more seconds before pulling back and lifting her gaze to Walker's. She saw something unreadable in his eyes.

"It took me months to get over her, to forgive her for leaving me like that. But you're right. What would have happened had we gotten married and then I decided I was done bull riding? Would we have gotten a divorce?" He shook his head, looking as though just the thought of that made him sick.

Lauren put her hands on his upper arms, trying not to register how toned they were as she looked up at him. The fire had died down some, and the light outside was dimmer than before, meaning it was either going to storm again or it was almost night.

"But look at what you've accomplished since. You didn't give up and just go back home. You invested in something that will keep you busy for quite a while. I would say that's a success all on its own." She paused, biting her bottom lip for several seconds. "And you got to choose what you wanted to do when you left the rodeo. Preston didn't really get that chance."

Walker's chocolate-brown eyes seemed as though they could see through her, and she realized she was holding her breath. Would he lean forward and kiss her, thereby sealing all of her dreams about him?

But instead, he nodded. "You're right. I wasn't forced to take over the family business, and for that, I'm grateful. But I'm still not sure how this venture will go." He lifted his hands a bit to motion to the rest of the room.

"Walker, just use the same grit you did in the arena and make it successful. You're not going to succeed just on wishes and hopes, just like you didn't become the best bull rider by sitting on the couch and watching TV all the time. Go for it; give it your all."

His stare became intense, and even with a flicker of his

lips upward, she found it hard to breathe. Of all the places she could have crashed after breaking up with her boyfriend, had this been some cruel twist of fate to end up trapped with the guy she'd wanted for most of her teenage and adult life?

He leaned forward, his eyes never breaking from hers. He drew close enough that their breath mingled together, and Lauren was sure he could feel her heart beating its way out of her chest. Was he going to kiss her?

Just as she was about to close her eyes, her phone began ringing on the couch behind her, breaking the moment.

Stepping away, Walker rubbed the back of his head and said, "I have to get some stuff done before dinner. But there are some things for sandwiches in the fridge. Bread in the pantry. Help yourself to whatever is in the house." He paused a moment before lowering his voice a bit. "Thanks again for your help with the, uh, business stuff. You're great at it."

He smiled and stalked over to pull some logs from the pile next to the stove and stoke the fire. When he walked outside, she let the phone go to voicemail as she watched the flames of fire lick the top of the stove, their movements reminding her of a dance.

She'd missed a phone call from one of her friends back in Colorado. Timing. It was always off in her life. But it was probably a good thing. She'd broken up with Cory a day ago. This was just a sign that she needed to take a step back and do what she could to make it through this storm without her heart breaking to pieces from lost hope.

It was good to be out in the cold air with his blood rushing as he lifted the heavy wet snow up and over his shoulder. Walker still hadn't been able to clear the entire driveway or the paths to the smaller cabins on the property, but with big spurts of progress, he hoped to be able to shovel most of the large drive in the hope that they could make it out of there when the roads opened again. Even to get the snow level low enough for the snowblower would help to maintain it with any future snow falling.

The clouds were a light gray, and the sky was brighter than it had been in days. He was just grateful for the break in snowfall and the chance to get his mind on something other than his best friend's little sister.

He still couldn't believe he'd told her all that, about his fear of failing at marriage. He'd shared stuff about his worries over an upcoming rodeo or trivial stuff like that with her in the past, but Lauren had been gone for so long. He shouldn't be spilling his deepest insecurities to her after they'd been together for less than a day. But there was something about Lauren that made him want to tell her everything.

As he thought about it, it was the sincerity on her face every time he spoke about something other than the mundane things, the look of focused concentration that wasn't pulled away by a phone or pretending to hear him and mumbling answers.

And he'd almost kissed her.

He'd never been around someone who believed in him so much, and the fact that she told him he'd be fine as long as he gave it his all helped to calm some of the anxieties that had been building over the last few days.

Walker couldn't get over the pull toward her. The girl who'd annoyed Preston for years had grown into a beautiful woman with a confidence she seemed not to realize she had. He'd never minded her hanging around and had always suspected she had some sort of crush on him, but he'd been so focused on bull riding that girls weren't even on his radar.

He chuckled as he thought about her reaction to Preston sabotaging her dating life in high school. It surprised Walker that she hadn't figured it out. But her brother hadn't had a chance to break up the relationship with her Fort Collins boyfriend as Lauren had never brought him home in all the time they'd been dating.

With how intense and perseverant he'd been in the past, it made Walker wonder why Preston hadn't just driven down and met the guy. Of course, the cows always had to be milked on schedule. And with their father's stroke and the boys' activities, it was difficult to get away for too long.

The door clanged behind him, and he turned to see Lauren trying to walk in some of his extra boots, probably a few sizes too big. She'd pulled on his extra coat, and it seemed to swallow her.

"What are you doing?" he asked, leaning on his shovel. He tried not to laugh as she maneuvered with the large boots.

"Well, there's a lot of snow out here," she said with arms stretched out and motioning to all the white. "I figured you could use some help clearing some of it. Do you have an extra shovel?"

Walker frowned. "You can go inside and relax. I'll be fine."

With her hands firmly planted on what he assumed were her hips under his coat, she raised her eyebrows. "My daddy would tan my hide if he knew I was letting you do all the work around here. Where's the shovel?"

Trying to suppress a smile, Walker motioned to the shed a few yards behind her. "In there is one."

She nodded with a grin and turned to get it.

Walker dug his shovel into another large mound of snow, pulling up what he could and throwing it onto the bank next to him. Now he wished he'd listened to Easton and gotten a snowplow installed on his truck for things like this. He had a small snowblower that was adequate for the sidewalks and smaller paths, but with the snow this deep, it probably wouldn't even turn over.

Lauren walked up a few feet to his left and started shoveling, her steady movements helping to keep him motivated. "It's been a while since I've done this," she said, a light laugh escaping her lips.

"I wish I could say the same. I'm sorry we're stuck in here. With getting the lodge ready for guests, I didn't think about snow removal."

"You're good. It looks like the roads are still closed anyway. Look, you can barely see my car." She pointed to the group of bare trees just inside the fence that ran around the property.

Walker took a step to the side and saw the headlights and a faint color peeking out from under a load of snow. "I'm sure glad you weren't hurt worse. The roads were so bad that the ambulance couldn't even get out here."

Her eyes widened. "Yikes." She gave him a small smile. "Thanks again for helping me."

"My pleasure." He winked and then grinned as her cheeks blushed pink.

They shoveled for several more minutes, then Walker turned to her. "You really don't have to do this. I feel bad you're even out here."

"Walker McBride, this is exactly where I'm supposed to be right now. Besides, it's good for me to get out some of the frustrations of not finding any jobs worth applying for."

"No luck, huh?" he asked, watching her as she continued shoveling. A pang of disappointment hit him that she hadn't said something about them being so close in the house, but he shook it off, knowing it was better to steer clear of the almost-kiss in the great room.

She dug deep, using her legs to lift the large load. For a small girl, she had no trouble moving the heavy snow. She leaned against her shovel, her breathing coming out in rapid spurts, the foggy cloud of air constant around her face. "Not yet. I'll find something. I guess the hardest part is that I did all this extra stuff at the insurance company, but I can't really prove it on a resume. But being here helps put things into perspective. I never should have been gone this long."

"You came for some holidays the past few years, right?" Walker offered.

With a quick nod, her expression fell. "Only a few since Mom's funeral and Dad's stroke. And I never enjoyed them. I was usually worried about what Cory was doing, and once the holiday was over, I'd rush back to Colorado, thinking I had to prove my worth to their company—well, more like their family."

"That's a sign that you don't want to be in their family,"

Walker said, his voice low. Emotions bit at his throat, causing moisture to form in the corners of his eyes. He'd felt like that with Cara's family, mostly because he kept beating Cara's brother in bull riding and it made him an outsider no matter what he did or didn't do.

Lauren rolled her eyes and laughed. "Well, I know that now. Being here has been so refreshing, like I don't have to be that cardboard cutout of the perfect girlfriend or employee anymore. I can just be myself."

She bent over and started shoveling again, and Walker did the same, turning so she couldn't see his smile. He knew what that was like, not having to walk on eggshells with what he said or did. Some things were more freeing than he could have imagined, even though being single was one of the hardest, most lonely things he'd ever done. But as much as it had hurt at the time, he'd come so far in the eleven and a half months since he'd given up bull riding that to go back would be to take those experiences away.

They worked in silence for a while, the only sound around being Bear playing in the bigger drifts. When they decided to go in, Walker turned to look at all they'd accomplished and smiled.

"You're a pretty good worker," he said as he admired how far they'd come.

"Why, thank you. You don't survive a family of four brothers by doing nothing all day." She grinned and walked past him into the house, her nose red from the cold.

Walker wiped some sweat from his forehead before following her in, feeling the wall of heat as soon as he opened the door.

After taking off his snow apparel, Walker walked into the gathering room and added some wood to the fire, as it was just a bit more than embers. Looking at the clock, he was surprised to see they'd been outside for almost two and a half hours, the longest stretch he'd been able to do since the big storms had hit. It helped that the temperature was more bearable.

"What do you feel like for dinner? I have a few jars of spaghetti sauce. Would that work?" Walker raised an eyebrow, waiting for Lauren's answer.

"Sounds great. That means I won't feel bad that you're slaving away for hours while I watch you cook."

Shaking his head, Walker said, "How about you help me chop some lettuce for salad? Then you won't have a reason to feel bad." He pulled a head of iceberg lettuce out of the fridge and set it in front of her. He grabbed the nearly new cutting board and chef knife and set them down next to the lettuce. "Chop, chop!"

Lauren laughed, the same deep sound as before, and Walker laughed along. "Are you sure you trust me with one of these? What if I cut my finger off?"

"Well, I patched up your forehead, so I'm sure I'd find something to help with the bleeding. Otherwise, you'll have to go without a finger." He leaned in a bit closer to look at the gash on her head, seeing just a slight red ring around it. "Looks like everything is healing well there." He pointed to her cut.

Lauren moved her hand up to feel it. "I almost forgot about it. I'm just glad it wasn't worse than that." She paused for a few seconds before unwrapping the lettuce from the cello wrap. "And I'm glad you were there to save me."

Chills ran up Walker's spine, and he gave a nervous laugh. "You're just lucky I know how to treat gashes like that. We've had so many of them in the McBride family that we should buy stock in a butterfly strip company." That got the both of them laughing so hard that tears rolled down Lauren's cheeks.

"How come I never knew you were this funny before?"

Her lips turned up in a mischievous grin. "Oh, because you didn't talk to girls back then, or really anyone but Preston."

He knew she was right, but he couldn't stop the next comment from slipping through his lips. "I'm pretty sure I talked to you and without Preston present, so that should count for something."

Her mouth dropped open, and the air left Walker's chest. Had he said too much? He didn't breathe again until she started laughing, looking down at the lettuce and nodding.

"Touché, Walker. Touché."

*L*auren focused on cutting the tomato Walker had given her after the head of lettuce, making sure not to squish it as the knife struggled to slice through it. The look on his face after he'd said he talked to her when they were growing up sent butterflies circling through her stomach. It was a mixture of trust and adoration, and she found it yet another difference from Cory.

She reflected on all the work they'd done that day shoveling snow, and even though he'd worn a coat, she could imagine his strong muscles flexing with every shovel of snow he threw. She glanced over at him now, admiring the long-sleeve shirt that emphasized his strong frame.

"Sorry, use this knife for that," Walker said, handing her a knife with a serrated edge. His words made her jump, causing her cheeks to heat. Hopefully, he hadn't seen her staring at him.

She pulled the blade against the skin of the tomato, surprised at how much easier it cut through. "How'd you learn stuff like this?" She pointed to the knife with her left hand and then grabbed the tomato again, readying herself for the next slice.

"Watching my mom cook, and when we were on the road a lot, we just had to learn to cook here and there. Mom wasn't with us when we traveled all that often, so we had to make do." He lifted one corner of his mouth in a grin. "You picked up some culinary skills from your mother. I remember you making the best apple pie when we were younger."

Lauren turned a bit so he couldn't see her expression, but she was sure he could hear the beat of her heart pounding against her ribcage.

"I forgot about that. I was so excited that I didn't burn it and people liked it. For some reason, the rest of the time I cook, it just doesn't sink in. I read a recipe a hundred times, and it still ends up wrong. I'll forget an ingredient or cook it too long. My mom could pull things from cupboards and the fridge, no recipe in sight, and the results would be amazing."

"I can understand that. The great thing about spaghetti is you can't really ruin it. Cook the noodles, brown some meat, and heat up the sauce. Butter some bread and toast it for a minute—" Walker's eyes went wide, and he turned to the oven, opening it to a thin cloud of black smoke. He pulled out a tray of charred bread and set it on the burners next to the sauce. "Or forget about it and make it black."

His face turned apologetic, and all the while Lauren was trying to keep from outright laughing. "I'm so sorry. It's just so funny how you—" She giggled. "That was a good one."

Walker pulled some plates from one of the cupboards and brought them to sit at the end of the large island. He carried the sauce and noodles over and then retrieved some salad dressing from the fridge for the salad Lauren had just cut up. With it all spread out, it was a grand feast for the two of them.

Once they filled their plates, Lauren twirled her fork in the pasta, watching Walker carefully pour dressing over the lettuce, a thin drizzle made in long lines back and forth. He was a puzzle, but the more she got to know him, the more the pull to leap right back into a relationship was harder to resist. How was she going to make it out of here with her heart intact?

Surely a girl who had just broken up with her longtime boyfriend shouldn't have feelings this strong, right?

"So, tell me a story." Walker placed a forkful of salad into his mouth.

"A story?" Lauren asked, frowning a bit. What real story did she have to tell that they hadn't already talked about at some point? "I've got a story. One with a tragic ending. It's of a girl who missed Thanksgiving with her family, missed the brown gravy and the fluffy mashed potatoes, the homemade rolls and the juicy turkey."

"What about stuffing? Did this girl not sample her mother's stuffing?" Walker's half-smile caused Lauren to stop as she stared at his face. The temptation to lean forward and kiss him right then made her turn and focus on the spaghetti.

After a moment of composure, she turned and grinned at him. "No, this girl doesn't like stuffing. Thinks it's a waste of time to make."

After leaning back in feigned shock, Walker said, "I don't know. Your mother made pretty good everything. But then again, so does my mom."

"It's like they grew up in the same house or something. How do they make everything taste so amazing?"

Walker just shook his head, and Lauren continued with, "Cory's mom's food was subpar, what was left of it when I got through the line. There were just a lot of red flags I should have seen sooner."

Walker twisted his pasta around his fork and smiled.

"Well, just know I probably ate your portion as well. Preston and I practically had to roll ourselves away from the table."

Lauren shook her head and rolled her eyes. "You say that, but I'm sure you both worked it off within a few hours."

"Guilty." Walker grinned, raising his hand. "My mom sent me home with some leftovers because she made two turkeys this year since your family was joining us. I ate them at about eight that night. You're lucky I even heard you crash into the fence. I was in a turkey coma at that point."

The look on his face was half-serious, and Lauren tipped her head back and laughed so hard that she started coughing and wheezing at the same time. Walker lightly tapped her back, but the tingle to his touch surprised her, and she had to stand up. Taking a long drink of her water, she did her best to compose herself.

The rest of the dinner went about the same, with them bantering back and forth about different topics or stories about things they'd been through, and Lauren couldn't remember a better night, especially not any of the dates she'd ever been on. Not that this was a date. This dinner was just two friends trying to survive being stuck indoors, she told herself, even though every part of her called liar.

The snow kept falling Saturday, and Walker wondered if it was going to quit anytime soon. They'd lost power for a few hours that morning, but luckily, it had come on quickly, and with the wood stove, they didn't freeze. While he loved having a reason for Lauren to stay with him, he also kept looking at the calendar, wondering if he'd be able to get all the orders he needed before people started coming to stay at Silver Brook Lodge.

He and Lauren had made significant progress on the large drifts of snow in the driveway, and Walker would make sure to snow-blow it after a few inches so they wouldn't have to shovel it all out again every time. They'd also freed his truck from its white prison, and he was just glad to hear it start with the freezing temperatures. The road still hadn't been plowed, so they wouldn't make it far, but at least that much had been accomplished.

She'd asked him for a tour in between bouts of shoveling, and he'd been more than excited to show her through the place. The front of the lodge opened into what would be the check-in desk and then the great room, with vaulted ceilings and the rustic look of a cabin. Stairs leading up to the rooms on the second floor began at the other end of the great room.

The kitchen and restaurant were located down from the reception desk and connected to the kitchen was the large cultural hall he hoped would be well-used. There hadn't been large gathering areas for weddings and special events in the valley since the original had burned down, and it was his intention to make that much easier on the people from Cold-water Creek.

Lauren had oohed and aahed through the entire tour, causing his heart to swell. He'd been proud of how it turned out, as had his family and friends, but for some reason, seeing her eyes light up as he showed her his hard work held so much more weight.

He glanced at Lauren sitting at the other end of the couch tucked under a blanket. It had taken her longer to get warm this time as they'd spent longer outside that afternoon. A strange sense of accomplishment filled him, like if he had her by his side, he could conquer the world.

They'd turned on a movie, one of the several his family had donated for the future guests of the lodge, and Lauren had been more than happy to choose a romantic comedy. Walker secretly liked this one and was grateful it hadn't been some of the others his sisters had made him watch over and over again when he lived at home.

"Are you okay?" he asked after seeing Lauren shiver, her whole body moving in response.

Her teeth chattered a bit. "Just trying to get warm." She smiled at him, her jaw quivering.

"Come sit here. Maybe I can help with that." He patted the seat next to him and stopped, realizing how forward that sounded. "I mean, uh, well, if you want." Mentally kicking himself, he turned to the screen so he didn't have to watch the decision play across her face.

A few moments later, the cushion next to him shifted and the blanket Lauren had been using draped over him. She curled up with her head next to his chest, and he draped his arm around her. For several minutes, he was stiff, like if he made any movement, he'd scare her away. But as the movie played and he heard her laughter at several points, he relaxed, wishing this could last forever.

"Thank you for all your help with the snow. I wouldn't have made it as far without you." He looked down, breathing in the floral scent of her hair.

She didn't shift but said, "I doubt that. It's not like I can move mountains like you." She poked in his side, and he jerked back, a ticklish reflex. She poked again, and he moved again, trying to slide away from her hand. "Don't tell me the fearless Walker McBride is ticklish."

"Maybe," he said, trying to keep his lips closed so he wouldn't laugh.

She reached out and tickled his side, causing him to fall off the couch. After several seconds, when to the point where he could no longer breathe, he raised his hands in surrender "Stop." His chest heaved.

Lauren sat back on the couch, giggling so hard she'd doubled over.

"How did I not know you were that ticklish?" Her white teeth and wide smile caused Walker to stare for a moment, the realization hitting him that he hadn't been this happy in so long.

He sat back on the couch and watched her, waiting for her to attack, but she scooted over and cuddled up next to him again, making him breathe out a sigh of relief. It was the most right thing in the world to have her in his arms.

He'd never really thought of her as more than his friend's sister, but she'd always been nice to him. Preston had always been annoyed by her, complaining to their parents that she kept tagging along.

But now, his chest was going to explode with happiness, the loneliness he'd gone through the past year seeming to be swallowed up with her presence.

The movie ended a while later, and the credits began to roll, but Lauren didn't push away from him. He was sure she could hear his heart pounding, and the smell of her vanilla shampoo kept him entranced.

Once the credits were over, she shifted a bit, sitting up next to him but still leaning into him. "Thanks for watching that with me. I needed a good laugh after all this week has dealt me."

Walker barely registered her small smile, focusing more on her eyes searching his face. The two of them were so close, inches apart, and as much as his brain told him to back up and give her some space, his head leaned closer, inch by inch.

The ping of a text message pulled him back a bit, and he reached into his pocket to pull his phone out. "It's Preston."

A feeling of dread looped through him. He'd been by Preston's side several times when he'd intimidated one guy or another into steering clear of Lauren. And here Walker was, nearly kissing her.

Hey. I just heard Lauren made it to your place. I'm glad she's somewhere safe. Take care of her until she can make it through the storm.

Preston would probably never think Walker would make a move on his younger sister, so he wasn't much of a threat.

Sure thing, Walker texted back.

"I'm not surprised that he's checking on me." Lauren smiled.

"Yeah. He's always been worried about you." With a long

sigh, he said, "We should probably get to bed. I'm beat after a day of shoveling."

"Me too," Lauren said, leaning against his chest again, not making an attempt to leave her spot.

They sat there for several moments, and he recognized the slower breathing on her end. Should he wake her and help her to bed? He'd carried her from the car the other night, so it wouldn't be that hard to help her to her room.

"A few more minutes," he whispered, breathing in her scent. But he didn't make it that far before his own eyes closed and he was dreaming of fulfilling the urge to kiss her.

CHAPTER 13

Lauren's dreams featured Walker as the leading man that night, and when she woke up the next morning with her head against his chest, she couldn't help but smile. She'd been disappointed when the text had come through from her brother, breaking off the one chance she'd probably ever have of kissing Walker.

But, maybe she'd dodged a bullet. She doubted things could work out long term between the two of them, especially with Preston's nose for any increasing feelings she'd ever had toward another guy. He'd always known she had a thing for Walker, but since Walker had never pursued her, he was a non-threat.

He was going to kiss her, though, right? She hoped it wasn't just another facet of one of her dreams.

He was still sleeping, a slight snore sounding from him, and she grinned. Getting up, she made her way to the kitchen, wondering if she could return the favor of making a meal. There was one thing she'd actually mastered with the help of one of her roommates at college.

Pulling out eggs, milk, and several other mix-ins, she

prepared to make him an omelet. It wasn't the fanciest thing ever, but it was something she never burned, and that was saying something.

She had just flipped it over to cook the other side and add the ham, peppers, and cheese when she heard footsteps behind her.

"Smells good in here. What are you making?" Walker leaned with his back against the counter, folding his arms as he grinned at her, his eyes still not quite open.

"An omelet. Is there something here you'd prefer not to have in yours?" She waved to the small piles of ingredients she usually enjoyed in her own.

He frowned, making a face that had her wondering what she'd done wrong. "I'm actually allergic to tomatoes."

Lauren's eyes went wide. "Oh, well, I'll eat this one and make you one sans tomatoes." She looked up as his chest started shaking with laughter.

He smirked. "Sorry, bad joke. I'm not really allergic to tomatoes. We had spaghetti for dinner, remember?"

His mischievous grin caused irritation as well as swooning to swell inside her, and she balled her hand into a fist, punching his shoulder. "Not funny. I was trying to return the gesture, and here you are, teasing me." She held up the spatula as if she would inflict more damage on him with it.

He raised his hands in retreat and scooted back a step. "Truce. I've been hit by those a few times, and they leave a mark." He motioned toward the spatula and laughed. "It was my mother's weapon of choice when we were eating before the food was done. All in fun, of course."

Lauren slid the omelet onto a plate and added the lightly toasted bread from the toaster. She placed the plate on the counter in front of him. "I'll let you butter those while I get this next one cooking."

A few minutes later, she had her own omelet plated and her toast spread with butter and homemade strawberry jam. She slipped into the chair next to Walker's and looked over at him.

"How is it?" She held her breath, hoping he would be honest with her about it.

"It's not very good. I don't think you should eat yours either." He stuck out his fork to steal the bite she'd just cut.

She laughed, swatting his hand away. "Not funny."

"It's delicious. See, you have some skills in the kitchen after all." He grinned at her before biting off a piece of toast.

She loved the sound of his voice, especially when he was complimenting her. "Thank you. What's on the agenda for today?"

Walker turned to look out the window. "Well, the snow just keeps falling, so probably some more shoveling as well as cleaning up around here. I wish I had all the things I need to install here already, but I'm sure there is plenty I can get done while we're snowbound."

"You mean 'we.' You've been kind enough to let me stay here and eat your food. The least I can do is help out."

Once they finished eating and did the dishes, Lauren ran up the stairs and pulled on some sweats and a long-sleeved t-shirt she'd had since college. She took the stairs a few at a time and jumped off the bottom step. It was something she'd done forever ago as a child, and she'd forgotten how much she loved it.

She heard a rustling sound from the hall. "Where are your cleaning supplies?" she asked Walker as he pulled on a coat. "There are some places I can work to clean inside, as well as plenty of dusting in the great room."

"You really don't have to do that. You're a guest of my hotel and should be relaxing."

Shaking her head, Lauren said, "I'm an old family friend

and will not take no for an answer." She bit her tongue before she could expound on wanting to be more than just a friend, reminding herself that a couple of days and one night of cuddling didn't mean he felt the way she had since grade school. Although, the feelings she'd always had for Walker were now growing exponentially, and soon enough, she was going to come down from the clouds and realize it was all a wonderful dream.

After he showed her where the supplies were, she turned on some music on her phone and worked systematically throughout the great room, making sure to dust several of the higher places using a ladder. Not many would notice it, but she liked getting all the little nooks and crannies cleaned. She just hoped the dust wouldn't return before Walker's opening day.

After some pauses for food throughout the day, she was more exhausted than she'd been in quite some time. But at the same time, she felt more accomplished than she had since she'd begun working for the Turners.

And when Walker helped her with some of the cleaning, a secret wish ran through her mind, the hope that she'd eventually be with someone as kind and as caring as he was…if things didn't work out with him now.

CHAPTER 14

Walker woke up Monday morning to Bear licking his hand. Scratching behind the dog's ears, he sat up, stretching as he did so. Sleeping in his bed was considerably more comfortable than his night on the couch, but he still preferred having Lauren in his arms.

The sun was a bit higher in the sky than he was used to, and checking his phone, he shook his head. Seven in the morning.

Preston's name appeared just below the time, showing a missed text. Guilt filled him. Now that his feelings for Lauren were growing, was he going to feel like he had to cover his tracks every time his best friend talked to him?

Hey, they said the roads should be cleared later today. I can come help out at the lodge if you need. The cows should be good until tonight.

As much as he could use the help with the last few things before people started showing up in just over a week, he wondered how it would work to have Preston and Lauren under the same roof, even for a few minutes.

Walker had never been a great liar, and after all she'd

done to help him out the day before, not to mention the light flirting and laughter they'd shared while working on his new dream, he wasn't sure he'd be able to keep his feelings from Preston. The lodge had seemed incomplete before she arrived, and now he didn't feel that deep loneliness he hadn't been able to recognize.

It was a chance he'd have to take. *Sounds great,* he replied.

Closing his eyes, he breathed out a sigh. He stood and pulled on some jeans and a long-sleeved flannel shirt. He wouldn't be going back to sleep, and Bear needed to be let out.

* * *

WALKER SIPPED his juice a little bit later while checking emails on his phone. The sound of a truck idling outside the lodge drew his attention. Preston must have been right about the roads clearing up, or the large delivery truck wouldn't be sitting in his driveway.

"Looks like the roads are clearing up, huh?" Lauren said from behind him, startling Walker. "I'm sorry. I didn't mean to scare you." She squinted to look out the window. "Is that a truck outside?"

Walker stood, stretching his arms high into the air and walked over to the door. "Yep." He opened it to see a large mound of boxes next to the front door and a large transportation truck pulling away. The one pathway they'd been able to clear had been beneficial because the last few décor items, as well as several fixtures, had finally shown up.

But a truck coming in meant the roads were now open. A sense of sadness ripped through him, as he knew there was no reason for Lauren to stay at the lodge when she could get back to her childhood home. It had been so lively here for the past few days, and somehow, she made this large building feel like home.

The text from Preston came back to mind, and he groaned inwardly. Walker had been awkward around Cara's family when they'd started dating, but how was he supposed to react with his best friend?

"Wow! That is a lot of boxes. Why do you have so many?" she asked, folding her arms across her chest as she looked out the glass front door. She looked so beautiful this early in the morning, and he was half tempted to kiss her again.

"Probably just built up from not being able to deliver for a few days." Walker shrugged and opened the door, pulling boxes in and setting them neatly against the wall.

Lauren picked up a box and mumbled something inaudible before she asked, "What is it all for?"

"The lodge. I had to order a bunch of things online since the hardware store in Afton either didn't carry the ones I needed or didn't have enough. I'm just hoping it's everything I ordered because there won't be much time before the lodge is officially open."

Taking a seat on the couch, Lauren tucked her feet underneath her and watched the growing number of boxes for another moment before Walker finished. "What made you decide to open so soon?"

"I know it's crazy to open right before Christmas, but I figure it can be a nice place for families to come for dinner for a change. You might not remember, but there aren't a whole lot of dining options in Coldwater Creek."

"Oh no, that I remember quite well. I usually grumbled about it when it was my turn to do the dishes." Lauren grinned, continuing to pull Walker in. He needed to be careful. Fix her a quick breakfast and then drive her to her dad's before his heart got sucked in too deep.

"Well, the roads must be open if the delivery truck made

it. Let me get you some food, and I can take you home." Maybe that would be the best way to deal with Preston coming. If Lauren wasn't here, he wouldn't have to worry about pretending that his feelings for her never existed. But if she was gone so soon, would she forget how it felt? Or did she even feel like that in the first place?

"Are you sure you don't need help with that?" she asked, pointing to the mound of boxes he'd just pulled in. "If you don't remember, I don't have a job at the moment and will have time to help if you need it. You just say the word."

Moving his gaze from her face to the boxes, a familiar twinge of guilt hit him in the chest. He didn't want her only memories of staying at the lodge to be of working. But he knew he wanted her there, wanted to talk to her just a bit longer before this small fairytale disappeared like a good dream. He'd take his chances on his acting skills when her brother came.

"If you're fine with that, I'd appreciate the help. Every little bit gets me to opening day."

She nodded, and his heart leaped. "I saw some bagels in the basket. Can I make you one, and we'll get working on all this?" She gestured to the pile of boxes sitting around them and raised an eyebrow, waiting for his answer.

"Sounds great. I'll take one of the plain bagels with straw-berry cream cheese."

Walker watched her walk away, smiling as he saw her graceful movements and wondering what a life with Lauren would look like. She was a lot more willing to help than Cara had ever been. More agreeable too. But he still came back to the fact that Lauren had listened to him talk about things every single time he'd needed it while they were growing up. That was a girl he needed by his side.

As they worked to open the boxes and figure out what contents came in which unmarked boxes, he tried to keep his mind on the fact that he had someone to help him and not on the fact that she might have been staying because she felt the way he did. He liked Lauren Burke, and the thought both thrilled and terrified him, even knowing that chances of things actually working out were slim.

She'd already mentioned something about needing time off from dating after her breakup, and here he was, hoping for a future together. The guilt sank deeper, like a large boulder pulling him down. What kind of a man was he to go around falling for a girl who'd just gotten out of a relationship?

"Go ahead and take those light switch covers into each of the rooms. I'll follow behind and install them." Walker motioned to the pile of covers sitting at her feet, each one designed with a bear, moose, or other animal on top of it to round off the nature themes of each room.

"I can do it. Just hand me the screwdriver, and I'll get started. You have that whole pile of fixtures to install still. We can work on each room together."

She smiled at him as he handed her the screwdriver and stuffed her pile of covers into one of the opened boxes, making it easier to carry. Walker picked up two of the ornate fixtures, not wanting to break anything by carrying too many at once.

They made their way upstairs and into the first guest room. It was the room Lauren was currently staying in, and seeing her luggage opened on the luggage rack and the bed hastily made sent some sort of warning through him, like this was her personal space and he shouldn't be invading it.

"Maybe we should start in the next room, and I'll get this one later." He shifted from one foot to the next, not daring to move over the threshold of the door.

"It'll be fine. Let me just throw a few things in my suitcase, and I'll get it out of the way so you can hang the fixture." She shoved several articles of clothing into the suit-case and moved the whole thing into the bathroom.

As she invited him in, it made him feel closer to her, trusted. He shook his head at the thought. He was reading way too far into it.

None of the rooms were customized just yet, as he'd been waiting for all the fixtures and décor to come. He was just glad some of the items had finally made it so he could focus on the final touches before the people who'd already booked rooms started coming.

"Do you have a system for which room is which theme?" Lauren asked, rifling through the covers.

"I'd planned for everything in each room to be the same, so moose light cover, moose fixture, moose décor."

She looked up at him, her expression blank. "But do you want this to be the moose room? Or bear?"

Walker searched his brain, trying to remember what he'd decided with his mother and sisters. They'd helped him a lot with the planning of the rooms, but with school and every-thing going on at the ranch, they hadn't been able to get out to the lodge much.

"I think this one is supposed to be one of the wolf rooms." Walker nodded as he remembered the sketch his younger sister had made of the lodge. With twenty rooms inside, he'd had to have multiple rooms the same, but that also made it easier to find the necessary décor.

"Perfect." Lauren pulled out a light cover and opened the package.

Walker watched as she walked over to the switch and started screwing the plate into place like she'd done this every day of her life. There was no way Cara would have done anything like that, even at the beginning of their rela-tionship.

Breaking his stare, Walker turned and moved quickly

back down the stairs, grabbing the small stepladder and running back up. He placed it under the wiring in the ceiling and focused on the work of connecting all the right wires so the fixture would be in place. He was lucky his father had taught all of his kids the basics of home remodeling when they were in their teens, giving him the knowledge to be able to do it himself and save some money.

It took about twenty minutes for him to install the fixture, making sure it was secure and that everything worked properly. He walked into the next room and found Lauren had already attached the light cover. He got to work again, grateful for her help and wishing he could find a way to have her stay longer than that afternoon.

CHAPTER 15

It was invigorating to help with all the small details of the lodge, and Lauren found herself pulling more and more items from the great room floor and taking them to the different rooms, making the beds in the ones that had a bed and doing her best to make things easier for Walker. She didn't need to be told where things went or what to do next, as she could figure it out as she went.

As each piece was brought into a room, it was as though a part of her was linking to the lodge like this was the place she was supposed to be. Shrugging that off, she knew it sounded ridiculous, especially since she'd just gotten out of a relationship. Their almost-kisses were on her mind at least every few minutes, and as hard as it was to push the thoughts away, she couldn't help but enjoy the memory.

Several of the rooms were near finished except for the fixtures and décor on the walls, but she'd have to ask Walker what he had in mind for those elements later. After wrapping up all the paper and plastic the items had come in, she took a couple of fixtures upstairs, placing them in rooms that still needed them.

She bumped into Walker on his way out of one of the bear rooms, and they laughed as they dodged back and forth, trying to let each other pass.

"Go ahead," Walker said, standing against the wall and waving her past with a wide smile.

Lauren grinned and raced down the hall, moving quickly to retrieve the last two fixtures and bring them upstairs. When she'd deposited them in their correct rooms, she moved back to where Walker was working and leaned against the wall in the room, staring up as his fingers connected the wires.

"I can't believe you know how to do all that," Lauren said, shaking her head.

Walker stood on the bed with his boots off as he worked, and she stared at the sight of his pants cut as if they were meant for him.

"I'm just glad you were able to get all the covers on. And that you made the beds and put a bunch of the little stuff out. This would have taken me a lot longer without you." He smiled at her before turning back to the fixture, sending Lauren's legs to feeling like jelly. She was just grateful she was already leaning against the wall so she didn't fall to the ground.

"What are you going to do about staff? You aren't planning on running this all by yourself, are you?" Lauren asked. Her feelings about the lodge had pushed the questions off her tongue. Maybe she could find a job here if nowhere else in Coldwater Creek.

Walker fidgeted with the light some more before opening his mouth to answer. But before he could say anything, the doorbell chimed, and they both froze, surprised by the sound. They hadn't had anyone by since the snowstorm, and it looked like a part of that solace was now gone.

"I'll go answer it. Maybe it's just another delivery truck."

Lauren took the stairs quickly and made it to the bottom stair where she could see the door. Her stomach dropped as she saw Walker's younger sister, Kassidy, as well as Preston behind her. Kassidy smiled with a curious look on her face.

Walker must have locked the door after bringing in all the boxes, because the deadbolt was done as well. Lauren unlocked them and threw the door open.

"Kassidy! It's been so long. How are you?" She took a step forward and wrapped her arms around the slightly taller girl.

When they pulled back, Kassidy said, "I'm good. But I'm a little confused as to what you're doing here." A sly smile crept over her face, and Lauren's cheeks turned to flames at what Kassidy must be thinking.

Preston didn't look quite as happy, his eyes narrowed and mouth taut. "I'm just glad to hear you broke up with the spineless Turner guy. At least that's what Dad said when he told us you'd been in an accident." His voice conveyed a bit of the betrayal he must be feeling since she hadn't called him, and Lauren knew she'd have to explain it all.

Pointing out the big window, Lauren said, "Well, if you'll notice my lovely car stuck over against the fence, covered in snow, I've been stranded for a few days. Walker pulled me out of my car, unconscious, Thanksgiving night, and he's been kind enough to let me stay in one of the upstairs bedrooms until the roads cleared."

"I'm glad you're okay, but you tried to drive from Colorado during that snowstorm?" Preston asked, the vein in his neck throbbing. He walked forward and pulled her into his arms, holding on longer than she was used to. Her irritation ebbed as she remembered how much he'd always protected her, and with their mom gone, he'd been even more protective.

Not willing to take any more of this, Lauren ushered them in the door and closed it behind them. Turning to her brother, she moved a few inches in front of him and stared up into his furious gaze.

"If you actually cared to know, I broke up with Cory and quit my job all in that same day. I just wanted to get home and spend some time figuring out my life. Is that okay with you?" She locked eyes with him, trying not to smile when she saw him backing down.

"I didn't know all that. I'm sorry, Laur. But if it makes you feel better, Cory didn't seem like the best one for you." Preston took off his coat and hung it one of the hooks just inside the door. Kassidy did the same, giving Lauren a hug as well.

"It's been a while, girl. How are you?" Kassidy whispered into Lauren's ear.

Pulling back a bit, she gave her old best friend a nod with a small smile. "I'm good. Just realized I wasted too long with the wrong guy." Looking up at Preston, his words about Cory seemed to stir up the old annoyance in her about what he'd done to so many other guys she'd had crushes on over the years.

"Well, it seems you don't think anyone is good enough for me, brother." She set her jaw and waited for him to retaliate. But instead, all eyes turned to the sound of someone coming down the stairs.

Walker grinned and walked forward, giving Preston a back-slapping hug. He then turned to Kassidy and gave her a hug as well. "Did you two come together?" he asked Kassidy.

"No," Kassidy said, her face lighting up like Rudolph's nose. "We just pulled up at the same time. I figured you could use some help around here to get things settled, but it looks like you've already gotten a lot done."

"She doesn't sass like you do," Walker said, chuckling as he pointed to Lauren.

Preston joined in, and Kassidy frowned at him, her lips pinched together like she'd eaten something bitter.

Preston walked to look at the great room. "What can I help you with?"

Lauren watched as Walker fidgeted, wondering what was going on with him. He was standing as far away from her as possible, and she wondered if that was a coincidence or intentional.

"I have a lot to get done out in one of the cabins. The rest of them should be good, but I haven't checked on them since the storm."

"Let's get to it, then. I have to be back by six to milk." Preston stalked back to grab his coat again.

As Walker grabbed his coat, Lauren walked up and touched his arm. "What do you have planned for Christmas decorations?"

He gave her a blank stare. "Um, I hadn't thought about that."

"Kassidy and I will come up with something for you. You'll need to have this place decked out for your guests to enjoy." She gave him a wide grin, hoping to feel the same way she had while they'd been in the lodge alone. Like there was some chance between them.

"I'd appreciate that. Thanks," he said briskly. He pulled on his snow hat and walked out the back door behind Preston.

So much for that.

"Let's go see what this place still needs," Lauren said, trying not to meet Kassidy's eyes. Her friend would be able to see right through her, and she didn't know what to make of the flip of events from last night to this morning. Part of her wished the snow hadn't been cleared so she could talk to Walker about what those almost-kisses meant.

CHAPTER 16

"It's been so long since we caught up. Are you back in Coldwater Creek for a while?" Kassidy asked.

Shrugging, Lauren frowned. They were in one of the upstairs rooms, and she was glad Kassidy hadn't brought up the question about what was going on between her brother and Lauren.

"I'm not really sure what's in my future yet. Since I quit my job and broke up with my boyfriend back in Fort Collins, things are pretty wide open at the moment. I've been helping Walker put up a bunch of the décor that came on a truck this morning." Wrong thing to say. That just led Kassidy right where Lauren didn't want to go.

Kassidy grinned, and something in her eyes made Lauren suspicious. The girl Lauren used to hang out with as a kid and a teenager leaned in and whispered, "So, is there anything going on between you two? I mean, I know how much you've always liked him, but it's been a while. And he's been through a lot over the past year. I'd like to see him happy." She winked, and Lauren wished she could disappear into a corner. She just hoped Kassidy couldn't see Lauren's feelings for Walker written all over her face.

"Kass, I just got out of a long relationship. It's probably not good for me to jump into another relationship so soon." At least, that's what she thought the sister of the guy she practically loved should hear right then.

Lauren turned to look at the windows, wondering if Walker had already ordered some kind of curtains. "What about you? What's new in your life these days?"

"So nice of you to ask, my devoted best friend."

Kassidy's sarcasm made Lauren's chest constrict. Yes, she'd been one of the worst friends ever since her mother died, but there was so much about Coldwater Creek that reminded her of her mother, including Kassidy, that it had been easier to stay away.

"The bank is still closed, so it's a snow day for me. As far as guys, there's no one in particular. I mean, it's a small town. Not much of a chance to find a good guy around here."

"So you're not still pining over my brother?" Lauren asked with a wink.

Kassidy reached out and punched Lauren in the shoulder. "That was forever ago. I know we used to dream of being each other's sisters through marriage, but I don't think Preston knows I exist more than an occasional hello."

Lauren nodded slowly, trying to get her brain onto the design track and off the handsome cowboy who was causing her insides to flip at every glance.

"Well, maybe we should just get a house and become old spinsters together. That's about how well my life is going right now." Lauren groaned, sad that all her dreams had come to this. She'd had so many a few years ago, but now that everything had failed, she didn't know where to start over.

"Come on, girl. You'll be fine. You just need to find something you love. I'm sure Walker could use some help. You're already helping him do some designing. Maybe you could do something with that. Just don't ask to be the chef." Kassidy widened her eyes and rolled her lips in, trying not to laugh out loud.

Shaking her head, Lauren took her turn to punch her friend in the shoulder. "I know I'm not a good cook, or even a cook at all. But I think I could manage the day-to-day operations of the lodge. I mean, insurance isn't even close to the hospitality business, but I went through enough junk at my last job to be prepared for quite a bit."

"Then ask him, or apply or whatever. It wouldn't hurt to try."

Blowing out a breath, Lauren knew she wanted to, but would that be the best decision? If a relationship didn't work out between them, she'd be left with the memory of two almost-kisses with the guy she'd been pining for longer than she cared to admit, all while having to see him every day.

"Yeah, you're probably right. I'll just ask and see." After looking around the room, Lauren turned to Kassidy and asked, "Has Walker ordered any art or paintings for the walls?"

Shaking her head, Kassidy said, "I don't think so. Are there any you can recommend?"

Turning on the art history major in her brain, she found she was a bit rusty, and nature paintings weren't something she studied a whole lot of.

"None off the top of my head, but I can do some research and let you know. What about a local photographer? Doesn't one of your brothers take pictures?"

"Yeah, Colter does. I haven't seen any of his pictures lately, but I could ask."

Lauren nodded. "I think some local pictures would be

better than anything professional. And maybe we could boost him into opening his own business."

Kassidy chuckled at that. "I'm pretty sure it will always be a side business. The rodeo takes precedence over everything for him." She glanced around the room again and said, "Then again, I never pictured Walker owning and running a lodge. I'll check with Colter and email some over, if he'll let me look at them."

"That would be great. I remember seeing some of his shots in high school, and he really had an eye for composition. A couple of proper frames would look amazing in the great room as well." The lodge would be ready for guests in no time.

Her thoughts turned to the lodge as a whole and everything that must have gone into building it. As much as she wanted to stay, she needed to get home, clear her head, and figure out what to do with her life.

"I should probably get back to my parents' house so I'm not bugging Walker anymore. Would you mind giving me a ride, Kassidy? I don't think my car is in any condition to make it anywhere right now." She bit her lower lip, her emotions jumbled inside her as she thought about leaving the lodge, and leaving Walker.

"I, uh, well, I'm not going home just yet, or I would. I have a few errands to run in Afton. But we'll have to do lunch or something to catch up while you're still in town. Are you coming to the NFR?" Kassidy asked, reaching in for a hug.

"I doubt it. Preston isn't in it anymore, and I should probably figure out what to do with my life before my savings run out." Lauren laughed, trying to remember the last time she'd watched her family compete at the National Rodeo Finals.

"Well, talk to Walker. A job here would be cheaper for you than down in Colorado. At least you'd save money on a place to live."

"A place to live? What for?" Walker asked, walking in with a slight smile on his face.

"I'm trying to convince Lauren to give up Fort Collins and move home. You should hire her as your manager. She'd be able to keep everything in order for sure," Kassidy said, looking around at the somewhat untidy room, causing Lauren to suppress a laugh. "Make sure to get Lauren home soon. I'm sure she's sick of the slave labor around here."

The grimace that crossed Walker's face was like a punch to Lauren's gut. Kassidy's bluntness surprised her. She'd had some sass growing up, but nothing like she did now. She said goodbye and walked out the door, leaving a strange tension in the air.

"I'm-I, uh, well…" Walker ran his hand through his dark hair, more flustered than she'd seen him in a while.

Closing the distance between them, Lauren rested her hand on his arm, squeezing a bit to reassure him. "I promise I enjoyed every minute, and I didn't feel like slave labor. It was nice to do something with design and something not involving insurance." She smiled wide, making sure he saw it.

"You're sure?" His uncertainty made her want to slip into his arms and hug him.

She hesitated before sliding her hands around his back and resting her head on his shoulder, feeling like they fit together like puzzle pieces. After several breaths, he relaxed and wrapped his arms around her, making her feel more safe and warm than she'd felt since she'd lost her mother.

She stayed there for several moments, listening to his steady heartbeat and breathing in the smell of his pine-scented cologne. She was sliding down a steep hill, and the more she tried to slow down the feelings inside her, the more the ground slipped beneath her feet.

He pulled back a few inches, and Lauren sighed, wishing the moment would have lasted a bit longer. "We're working to finish a few things in cabin eight, and then I can take you home. Will you be all right?"

Lauren looked up into his eyes and then to his mouth, the temptation to kiss him almost too great. But the spell of the moment completely broke when his arms slid from her back and he took a step back, giving her a small smile.

Tucking a section of hair behind her ear, Lauren nodded. "I'll be fine. There's plenty to do in here to get you ready for your guests."

Walker moved back to the door but stopped and turned halfway there. "Was Kassidy serious about you being the manager? Is that something you'd like to do?"

"I've never managed a hotel before, but I'm thorough and will make sure I know all about it if you give me the chance."

A broad smile covered his face. "You're hired. Just tell me what you need, and I'll take care of it." He paused a moment, appearing to wrestle with something before he nodded and walked out the door.

She was able to wait until several seconds after he'd left before cheering. She'd never been so excited about a job, and this one would be a good challenge for her. Plus, it would give her more time to be around Walker. Whether that was a good thing or not remained to be seen.

Now all that blocked her from settling back down in Coldwater Creek was her townhome in Colorado. If she could get everything moved back without running into Cory, her past would be officially behind her.

CHAPTER 17

Walker's breath hung in large clouds in the gray light. The temperature had dropped several degrees already, but it was afternoon, and it would only get worse that night. After starting his older Chevy truck, he walked back into the house, meeting Lauren at the bottom of the stairs.

"Let me take that for you," he said, taking the bags in one swoop without letting her protest. He went back to the mudroom door and set a bag down so he could hold the door open for her.

Preston had left a few hours earlier after several prying questions about what he and Lauren had been up to while snowed in. He'd also been ranting and raving about how Cory had been the worst thing for Lauren and that she really needed to get a new radar for guys.

What was a new radar supposed to look like? And would Preston think Walker qualified to be on it? Because more than ever, Walker hoped he and Lauren could figure things out and make them work. But he had time. He'd just hired her as his new manager, which felt so right. But at the same time, what if something went wrong?

With the direction of their conversation, Walker had never been so relieved to have his best friend called back to the farm for an emergency, and even with as much help as Preston had given him, Walker was grateful to see him go while Lauren was still busy inside, making it so Walker would have to drive her home.

"Thank you," she said softly, moving in front of him to the truck.

He helped her in before sliding her bags under the flat top bed cover of the truck. Hopping into the driver seat, he rubbed his hands together. "Sorry, I thought it would be warm already, but this weather is already getting colder."

"I'm actually quite warm." Her cheeks reddened, and Walker wondered what she meant by that comment. If it had anything with their embrace earlier, then he was fairly warm still too. He'd thought about reaching forward and kissing her, but Preston's words echoed over and over again.

The few-mile drive to the farm was quiet, the only sound a few of the country songs that came through on the two channels in this part of Wyoming.

"Uh, thank you again for all your help. It made things run a lot faster." He glanced over at her and then back at the road, knowing he'd probably steer off the road if he stared any longer.

"Thank you for rescuing me. And letting me help out, cooking me amazing dinners. It seems like I got the good end of the bargain." She chuckled, the sound causing him to breathe just a touch easier. He could probably listen to that sound every day for the rest of his life.

"So, boss, what time do you want me at the lodge tomorrow?" she asked.

Walker chuckled, laughing at the use of the word boss. He'd never been a boss over anyone, and for some reason, that made a zip of anxiety rush through him, settling into his chest. Would he be able to be the boss of several people, their paychecks depending on him? But that's what he'd hired her for.

Breathing out slowly, he said, "Eight, nine, whenever. Do you want me to pick you up until you can get your car fixed?"

She reached over and touched his hand. "Thank you, but I know you have a lot to deal with there. I'll borrow one of the ones at home or have a brother drop me off."

He pulled into the driveway of the Burke home, viewing it in a new light after the past few days. He'd always seen it as the home of his best friend, but now he realized how much of Lauren had been shaped there. How many times had she mentioned her upbringing since she'd come to the lodge? It made him wonder why he'd never taken notice of her like he did now.

"Come in for a minute. I'm sure my dad will want to thank you." She smiled at him before opening the door and jumping out.

The white snow with the warm yellow lights from the house made Walker smile. The Burke family was so much like his own that this was almost like coming home.

He helped Lauren up the few steps with her bags and onto the wraparound porch and then waited a few feet behind her as she knocked and rang the bell.

"Since when did they start locking things around here?" she muttered.

Walker bit his bottom lip so he wouldn't laugh.

Footsteps sounded on the other side of the door, and it swung open, Mr. Burke taking up a good portion of the doorway. "Lauren! It's so good to have you home." He pulled

Lauren into a crushing hug and stepped back, allowing them to enter the house.

Walker lifted the bags inside and stood up to see Lauren's father staring at him.

"Thanks for taking care of our girl. We always think our kids will listen to us, but sometimes they just think they're too big for our advice." He turned his eyes to Lauren, shaking his head.

"Come on, Dad. It had been a rough day, and I was just hoping to get home so I could be with everyone. But at least I didn't freeze to death out on the road." Lauren tilted her head to the side as if ready to battle him out on the issue.

Her father turned to look at Walker again. "Come in and get something warm in you. It's supposed to hit single digits overnight."

Walker waved and took a step back. "Thank you, Mr. Burke. I've got a lot to get done over at the lodge still, so I'd better head back."

"How's that coming? I'll be glad to have another restaurant in the valley again. Are you planning for it to be a steakhouse?" The man's bushy eyebrows rose, causing him to look almost cartoonlike.

"That's the plan. I just heard back from a chef this morning who has committed to coming, and I'm working to hire the rest of the staff and waiters and waitresses. So if you know of anyone who needs a job, send them my way." His gaze lowered to Lauren's, and he gave her a warm smile. "I already hired Lauren to be my manager."

Mr. Burke gave his daughter the brightest smile Walker had ever seen from the man, the wrinkles around his eyes nearly swallowing them. "You mean you got my daughter to stay in Coldwater Creek? I don't know how you did that, but I owe you, Walker. It's an early Christmas present." Her father shook his hand and thanked him again before

Walker said goodbye and walked out the door and into the cold.

Lauren followed him and closed the front door almost completely behind her as she stepped closer to Walker.

"Thank you again, for everything. I'll see you tomorrow?" A sly smile stretched across her face.

"I look forward to it." The words came out more breathless than he'd intended, but with the way she looked with her hair down around her shoulders and a smile accentuating her delicate features, he wasn't sure he was actually awake.

She stepped down from the door and drifted closer to him, their breath mingling together in the gray light. "And let me know when I can take you to dinner to thank you for all you've done. I promise we'll have someone competent enough to not burn everything."

Walker laughed as he studied her face, his eyes moving back and forth from her eyes to her lips, all while his emotions lumbered between wanting to kiss her and wanting to stay as far away as possible from breaking his heart. He couldn't go through that again.

"Let's get some people hired, and then we can figure out a time. I'd like that."

"That's fair. See you in the morning." She reached up on tiptoe and kissed his cheek.

Walker stiffened, surprised by the blossom of electricity that branched out from where her lips touched his skin.

Lauren pulled back with a smile and returned to the house.

His heart began pumping faster and faster in his chest. Maybe if they took things slow, a relationship between the two of them could work out. He just hoped it wouldn't end like his last one.

After climbing into the truck, Walker sat immobile for several moments as he processed everything that had happened that day and the days leading up to it. He was twenty-eight, old enough to make a decision about who to like. He shouldn't be worried about his best friend's opinion of Walker's feelings for Lauren. But this was all new and so much more powerful than he thought it could to be. And his relationship with Preston was one of the things that had gotten him through the last year.

He'd just need some time to figure things out and see where it went.

CHAPTER 18

*W*hile it had been nice to get home to the farm for the night, Lauren was surprised to find how much the lodge already felt like home once she pulled into the driveway on Tuesday morning. With all the tasks she had to complete with only a week to go before opening day, she was grateful to have a challenge before her.

As the day went on, she was disappointed that she wasn't able to spend much time with Walker. He was always out fixing something or making sure to clear the large driveway and parking lot of snow. There hadn't been any more big storms since the weekend before, but little flurries continually passed over the lodge.

By Thursday, she was getting a handle on all the aspects of the lodge. Walker had given her access to the email and reservations, which helped her figure out what still needed to be done. When she wasn't answering phones or doing stuff on the computer, she was busy hanging some of the Christmas decorations she'd bought in town the afternoon before.

The lodge was taking shape, and she could see why

Walker was so excited but also anxious at the same time. There was a lot riding on this, and while she didn't know how much he had in the bank from his time as a bull rider, she knew this venture had probably taken a lot of funds already.

Friday morning, she checked the email only to find a headline that didn't look right. Opening it, she read the contents of the email, her stomach dropping.

Dear Mr. McBride,

I apologize for the late email after confirming I would be able to be the chef at your lodge just this past Monday. I regret to inform you that I will no longer be able to work for your lodge as I've received an offer that will allow me to live in my current home. I wish you all the best this Christmas season, and if I can think of anyone, I'll send them your way.

Sincerely,

Chef Tom Watkins

Lauren's mouth dropped open. They'd been able to secure housekeeping staff and several waiters and waitresses over the past few days. Lauren had done several interviews and extended the offers, which seemed to make the burden on Walker much easier. But the fact that they no longer had a head chef to direct the other cooks in the restaurant? That wasn't going to help things.

Slipping on her coat, she walked outside to find Walker. The search took longer than she expected, but she finally found him sitting on a log by the river that ran next to the property. Bear was curled up next to him on the cold ground.

"What are you doing clear over here?" she asked.

He jumped and turned toward her, and she felt bad for interrupting his thoughts.

"Just thinking. Thanks for all you've done this week. Hiring you has been the best thing I've done so far with this lodge." The corner of his lips ticked up and down so quickly that Lauren wondered if she'd imagined it.

"Don't thank me just yet. We just got an email from the chef. He's not coming." She tried to deliver the news gently, but from the terror in his eyes, this was Walker's worst nightmare.

He stood, brushing the snow off his pants and moving closer to her. "Not coming? What do you mean 'not coming'?"

"He said he received an offer closer to home and decided to take it so he didn't have to move." She paused a moment, letting the information sink in. "Were there any others who expressed interest in coming here?"

Walker rested a hand on his hip, the other hand combing through his hair. "Not yet. I should have put out the ads months ago. Why didn't I do that?"

Lauren stepped forward and took his hand. "We'll be okay. It's nothing we can't figure out."

"If we don't have a chef, we don't have a restaurant," he snapped. His voice hadn't risen in volume, but the tone cut.

Lauren dropped his hand and took a step back, reeling from his comment. She made the conscious decision not to react. It was a strange parallel to something Cory would have said to her, although Walker's statement wasn't a backhanded comment. But this was a side of Walker she hadn't seen before. She hoped she could just chalk it up to stress or anxiety over the opening of the lodge.

"We've still got several days. We'll think of something. I'm going to head back inside and check on a few things." She turned sharply and took several steps in the now crunchy snow before she stopped and said, "Let me know if you need to talk or need help with anything out here."

She blew out a breath, hoping to get this chef thing under control before the guests began arriving on Tuesday. There were a lot of people anxious to be at the restaurant on opening day, and she didn't want to see Walker feel like a failure after everything he'd done so far.

He'd been so distant the past few days, like he was avoiding her. Was he second-guessing getting too close to her? She'd have to find a time to ask him because she wasn't going to be walking on eggshells the rest of the time here.

CHAPTER 19

Walker sat back down on the stump, shame washing over him. He should never have said something like that to Lauren. He'd been so wound up over the past few days, nightmares coming about the failure of the lodge and the restaurant or, worse, that it burned down again. After all he'd put into this place, he just didn't want to be seen as a failure.

Not that he'd failed in the rodeo, but the fact that most people saw him as a has-been was difficult. It was normal to fail at some things, right? He just wasn't sure he'd be able to do that and still survive.

And if he was a failure with the lodge, would Lauren stick around to watch it all come down? Or would she move on like Cara had?

Shaking his head, he knew he needed to apologize. He'd barely spoken to her over the past few days, everything seeming to come to a head inside of him, and he wasn't sure whether or not it would all work out. He wanted to have the hope and optimism she had, but this was something he'd never dealt with, never worked on before. The only reason he'd gotten a loan for the place without any prior experience was because he brought enough money to the table that the bank deemed it acceptable.

Lauren had done an amazing job interviewing and hiring people all week, and he sent up a silent prayer, thankful she'd been sent to him. He wouldn't have been able to get all that done in just a few days' time, and she hadn't even asked him to talk about wages.

He didn't deserve her, just like Preston had said about all the guys in her life. But he held a sliver of hope that after all of this settled, he'd be able to figure things out with her. Would she even want him after how he'd been acting the past several days?

The real question was, could he bear to lose her? She'd brought more life back to him in just a few days than Cara ever had, and if he didn't have Lauren in his life, he wasn't sure how hard it would be to come back from that.

"I think I'm making a mess of my life, Bear. What do you say to that?" He looked down at his dog, whose eyes were barely open as he watched the icy landscape in front of them. "But I think I love her."

The thought overwhelmed him, and a warm sensation seeped through his limbs, as if signaling he was right.

Bear grunted, and Walker smiled. Nothing like a dog to put him in his place.

* * *

As HE WALKED INSIDE, Walker was amazed by the amount of Christmas decorations already hung in the great room. He looked through all the rooms and kitchen, hoping to find Lauren somewhere so he could apologize. He found her standing on the front porch, staring out at the mountain and the road in front of them.

Her car had been towed away on Monday night, and she'd said something about them totaling it, but he hadn't taken the time to talk to her about anything other than the business in the past few days.

He stepped out onto the porch, and if she noticed he was out there, she didn't acknowledge it.

"Lauren, I'm sorry about out there. I shouldn't have been so blunt."

She turned to him, her usually green eyes appearing more dark gray in the low light of the cloudy afternoon. "Thank you for apologizing. I know this is a lot of work and it's your dream, but I'm trying to make it happen, trying to be a part of it too. So just know that I'm emotionally invested in this place as well." The hardness of her tone caused Walker to pause, surprised by her words.

He hadn't thought about someone else hoping for something just as much as he did, but it was nice to have someone to share the burden with.

"I understand. Any news? I know it's been all of ten minutes, but I was hoping some miracle would blow a chef through the doors." He smiled, hoping it would ease the hardness of her features. She gave him a courtesy smile and shook her head.

"No, nothing yet. There are some options of people in the valley who could cover for us until we find someone who will go full time." She licked her lips, drawing his attention to them.

As much as he wanted to kiss her to show her how sorry he was for snapping, he could tell from her rigid body language that now was not the right time.

Walker nodded. "Who are you thinking?"

"Your mom would be an excellent chef. She was up there with mine in winning awards every year at the county fair."

"She would be good, but she still has a lot going on at the

ranch and wouldn't be able to be gone for six-plus hours on a weeknight." Walker took a few paces to the side and walked back, hoping the movement would reveal someone they could use for a while.

"What about you?" Lauren's words stopped him in his tracks.

His head snapped toward her, trying to see if she was serious. "Me? A chef?"

When she nodded, he said, "I'd never survive. And I really don't know that much about cooking."

"You do, though. At least you'd be able to learn the menu and cook that. Keep it simple, and with the cook staff we've hired, you should have enough help to serve the fifty-plus occupancy restaurant." She gave him a knowing look, and the more he thought about it, the more he knew it was going to have to happen. What other options did he have to save the opening of his restaurant?

"We'll need to practice, then. Maybe get our families together so I can cook? We can have the staff come in early to make sure we get all the bugs out before opening day." His voice wobbled on the last few words, not truly believing he was agreeing to this. He would do anything to make this lodge work, not only for his own pride, but for the economy of the Coldwater Creek Valley.

"I'll make sure to call everyone and have them come in. Sunday would be best so we can order anything we're missing before Tuesday." She nodded and moved toward the door, brushing her shoulder against his.

He reached out and caught her wrist. "Is everything else okay?"

Lauren took a deep breath, as though she was trying to decide on an answer. "Can we talk later? After I make these calls, I mean?"

"Sure. You just let me know when you're ready."

She walked inside and shut the door firmly behind her.

What could be bugging her? Had his sharp words affected her that much? Was she upset that he'd been so distant this week? He just hoped he'd have the answers to give her when it came time.

She was a chicken. A big chicken. Why hadn't she just stayed out there and asked him all the questions that had been piling up over the past few days?

Because she didn't want to be hurt by the answers. Maybe everything she'd imagined about a future with Walker had all come because of time stuck together in the lodge. Maybe she'd just read into it all wrong, just like she had with Cory. That thought sank deep, causing an ache she couldn't ignore.

She'd never been good at relationships, but the way he'd been avoiding her since she'd started working for him gave her the impression that she'd just made up everything between them, playing on her teenage crush fantasies and believing something was there when it wasn't.

Well, she could be the stalwart employee and make sure this company ran better than Walker had ever imagined. She'd forget about them and mend her heart one day at a time, knowing that at some point, she'd be okay with how her life goals had changed over the years. It would all be worth it in the end. To have a rewarding career and get the chance to help plan the bigger events like wedding receptions and big family gatherings. Those were so much more rewarding than having to file insurance claims.

But this was how her life was going to be. She just needed to steel herself from feeling anything for her boss, knowing it wouldn't work out anyway. It seemed like his injury and former relationship still had somewhat of a hold over him, even though she didn't know the complete story there.

Picking up her phone, she dialed Kassidy, knowing she needed something to do that night to get her mind off Walker. Kassidy picked up after the first ring, and Lauren was grateful.

"Hey, friend. What's up?" Kassidy said.

"What are you up to tonight?" Lauren asked. "I'm dying to do something."

"A bunch of us are going to Bridgerton to the karaoke club there. Want to come?"

Karaoke wasn't one of Lauren's strong suits, but she was ready for anything that would help her forget that today had happened.

"Sure. Just let me know what time."

Hanging up, she was grateful for a friend to call who wouldn't even ask what was going on but just invite her along. She wasn't in the mood to talk about anything at the moment, and being a little silly might help her to remember why it was good she was moving back to Coldwater Creek.

* * *

KASSIDY PULLED into Lauren's drive in her large jeep, the one Easton and Walker used to drive in high school. The twins had saved up for their own cars, and Molly still hadn't gotten her license, but that was her own decision, being seventeen.

"Get in, girl. Let's go have some fun."

Lauren laughed as she jumped in, trying to be a bit more

ladylike with her knee length skirt and cowgirl boots. She hadn't worn the boots since she'd left for college, thinking she was over things like that when she was going to a big city. But deep down, these were her roots, and it was comforting to be sporting them again.

"You look good, girl. Better than the work clothes you wear around the lodge." Kassidy had visited for a minute on Wednesday, bringing over several prints of Colter's photos. They were amazing, and just like she'd remembered, he was able to capture some of the most breathtaking moments.

"What is the manager of a hotel supposed to wear? A cowgirl hat and spurs?" Lauren joked, leaning back as Kassidy took off down the highway.

"No, you'd look ridiculous in that. What I'm saying is you should tone it up a little bit. All black makes you look like you should work at a mortuary or something."

Lauren sighed. "That was one day, all right? I haven't gotten everything from my apartment yet, so I'm trying to make do with what I have."

"I'm just playing, girl. How are things with Walker?" She wiggled her eyebrows and grinned at Lauren, causing a pit to form in Lauren's stomach. She'd rather go back to talking about wardrobe than this.

"Well, I think we're back to the same state we were in while we were in high school. I must have imagined everything before I left the lodge—"

"Wait a minute." Kassidy cut her off, her shock making Lauren realize what she'd said. "Do you still like him? You better spill, or I'm going to have to ask him about it."

Lauren closed her eyes, wishing she'd decided to stay in and do nothing but binge-watch a TV show or something. Then she wouldn't have to divulge all the humiliating things in her life. No, liking Walker wasn't humiliating, but the length of her crush on him was. She'd held a little torch for him for at least fifteen years. Was that why she'd never had a good relationship?

Shaking her head, she laughed. She'd had one relationship, and that was with an idiot who didn't know how to treat a woman.

"Yeah, I like him. But spending that much time with him only made things worse. He's going to think I'm Preston's younger sister until I die, and all I want is for him to see me as a possibility. Take a chance, you know?"

"So, have you kissed yet?" Kassidy asked and then held up a hand. "Wait, I don't want to know that. He's my brother, and there's only so much I need to know."

"There was an almost-kiss, or two...or three. But of course, my brother had a part in ruining it by texting. There were so many sweet moments with Walker that I was sure he was beginning to feel the same. But he's been avoiding me, and then he snapped at me when I told him the chef wasn't coming anymore."

"Jerk. I'll have a talk with him."

Lauren waved her hands at Kassidy. "No, don't. He already apologized. Maybe I'm just really bad at reading guys. Maybe he never really had feelings for me and things just got complicated because we'd been together for a few days."

It was quiet for several minutes before Kassidy asked, "So, what are you going to do about it?"

"What can I do? I'll just keep working and make sure to avoid him too. Then I won't go thinking he likes me when he really doesn't. But I love the lodge. I love working there and the challenge of keeping everything straight. I think it would be hard to leave even though I've only been working there a week."

"What about talking to him?" Kassidy asked, her eyes narrowing in on the road.

Shame rushed through Lauren. What could she say? "Well, I've thought about that. He even asked me what was wrong today, and I told him I'd talk to him later. Then I ducked out before he came back in from working on one of the cabins."

"You chicken! How are you ever going to know the truth if you don't ask?"

"I know, I know. But there's a small part of me that wants to cling to the hope that he likes me." Lauren opened her small purse, trying to find something to occupy herself with until they made it to Bridgerton twenty miles away.

"I understand that one. I think that's how I feel about your brother, like there's still some minute chance he'll look at me like he can't go another day without me."

Lauren reached over and touched her friend's arm. "Oh, Kass. Let's go have the best night ever and not worry about boys. Just like the good old days."

Kassidy chuckled and pushed the gas pedal, sending the jeep hurtling forward. This was going to be a night they wouldn't forget.

CHAPTER 21

Walker had come in around five, his stomach roaring with hunger after a long day of working. Things were slowly coming together, and he knew it would only be a few more days before he would know if all his efforts over the past twelve months had been worth it.

One thing he was grateful for was the work around the place that kept him active. He hadn't been able to do much for the first few months of owning the property, but it had worked out with the contractor starting the plans and getting it ready to go.

Lauren was nowhere in sight, and when he glanced outside, the old beat-up truck she'd been driving around the past week was gone. Did she really have something to talk to him about? He wished he'd insisted that they talk then, because the suspense of it was killing him.

Deciding he needed to get out of the house for the night, he drove over to the ranch, knowing most of his family was probably still out doing chores. He walked in and left his hat and coat on the coat rack just inside the door. Making his way into the kitchen, he could smell his mother's garlic mashed potatoes, and his mouth watered.

"Hi, Mom." He took a seat on one of the barstools facing the stove and grinned at her.

"Well, if it isn't my son that never visits me anymore." She winked at him and laughed. "How's everything coming at the lodge? Is there anything I can come help you with tomorrow?"

Walker thought about it, trying to mentally go through all the rooms to determine what still needed to be done. "I'm not sure yet. Let me text you when I get back tonight."

"What brings you here tonight?" His mom turned and leaned over the counter, always good at making eye contact and taking the time to talk.

But Walker wasn't sure he wanted to talk. He'd just needed something different than the lodge, where he'd been working and sleeping for the past four months. It was exhausting trying to get all the little things done, but his contractor had agreed to let him do some of the final work, which helped save a little money.

"Just needed a break. And if I stay at the lodge, I feel guilty for not working on every little thing."

She smiled and reached her hand out to him. "It's okay to have a little fun, you know." Taking a step back, she stirred something in one of the pots on the stove. "Kassidy told me you hired Lauren Burke to be your manager. How's that going?"

All sorts of complicated is what he wanted to say. "Going well. She's very organized and has already gotten the place halfway decked out for Christmas. I was thinking I need to go cut down a tree for the great room. With the vaulted ceiling, a big tree will top it off."

"That's a good idea. Take Lauren with you. I'm sure she'd have a good eye for what would work."

It was a good idea, and he tucked it away so he could remember to call her once he left the ranch. That would be something fun for the two of them to do to ease the tension before opening day.

As he sat there, he started thinking about his mom and dad and how they'd gotten together. His mother had been from a family of five boys and herself, and he wondered if any of them had been like Preston.

"Were your brothers really protective of you, Mom?" he asked, twirling his key ring around his finger.

"Oh, yes. There were several times when I would catch them threatening a date I'd had the weekend before, and I finally figured out why none of the guys would ask me on a second one." She chuckled, her eyes far away with the memories.

"So, what did Dad do to get through that?"

His mom shifted back to the island, leaning against it as she poured out the water from the potatoes into the sink. After adding butter and milk, she began mashing the potatoes. The smell of the garlic hung heavy in the air.

"Well, Dad was best friends with Uncle Gary for all of high school. He'd moved to Coldwater Creek as a sophomore, and they'd just clicked. When Gary found out we were dating, there was a bit of a disagreement, but when Gary saw how happy I was, he finally gave in." She looked at him, and Walker could see the wheels turning in her head. "All I can say is if you feel something for her, the family will understand."

His mother, always so perceptive. But Preston came to mind. He'd have to find a way to break the news to his best friend, and it was what he'd been dreading since the moment he recognized his feelings for Lauren.

The back door opened, and in came the flood of the household, all of the siblings with red cheeks. The only one missing was Kassidy, but that wasn't unusual for her. She tended to do what she wanted when she wanted.

They all said hello, giving him a hard time for not coming by as often anymore, and they sat down to dinner. After grace, they ate the delicious steak and potatoes, homemade rolls, and fresh green beans from the garden. He was going to need more than just advice on love from his mother. He was going to need prayer and some good practice to make sure this next week worked out okay.

CHAPTER 22

*L*auren didn't see she'd missed a call until they'd gotten into the jeep and were heading back after a night of fun with a bunch of her old friends. They'd all changed in their own ways, but there was quite a lot that had stayed the same.

The missed call was from Walker at nearly eight o'clock. He hadn't left a voicemail, but she wondered what he could need.

Before she could dial his number, a text came through from her landlord in Fort Collins.

I've got someone to rent out your apartment starting next week. I'll need you to clear your stuff out as soon as possible.

Of course. She'd called him on Tuesday after her first day working at the lodge, knowing that this was where she wanted to stay. She'd told him she would wait until the end of the month to move out since she'd already paid, but she didn't have much of her wardrobe in Coldwater Creek, and it might be better to get it all now rather than wait until after the holidays. She'd have it all tied up and really be all-in for a new life here.

"What's with the look on your face?" Kassidy asked, finally sliding into the driver's seat. She'd been talking to a cute guy from Jackson for most of the night, and while Lauren didn't mind, she was ready to get home and get to bed.

"What's that look on yours? Seems like mission accomplished on the 'Forget Preston Operation.' That guy was cute." Lauren nodded out the window in the direction the guy had gone.

"Yes, he is. But he lives in Jackson. We'll see if he calls."

Lauren frowned, not getting the connection. "What's wrong with Jackson?"

Kassidy gave her a look of disbelief as she turned the key in the ignition. "It's winter, and there are a ton of ski bunnies up there looking for guys to hang out with. I'll just be a quick memory." She said the last sentence with her voice rising so high that Lauren laughed out loud.

"I don't think you'd be a quick memory to anyone, Kass. You're definitely the life of the party."

"Not always. I just needed tonight. Lots of decisions coming up, and it's nice to get out all the worries with a night out with a bunch of girlfriends." She pulled out of the parking spot and started the drive down the highway back to Coldwater Creek.

"What kind of decisions?" Lauren didn't want to pry, but if she was going to be living back in her hometown, she should probably start being the best friend Kassidy deserved.

Kassidy sighed. "The bank is going through some restructuring, and I'm hoping I get one of the spots left open from the people that leave. I could use a promotion from being a teller."

"But I thought it was perfect for your rodeo schedule? Don't they work around you for that?"

"I don't know how much longer I'll be doing that, Lauren.

Barrel racing used to be so much fun, but now it seems like it's more work than it's worth to get ready to go. I'm feeling an itch to try something new."

Lauren grinned at her friend. "Why not skiing? Get that guy to take you." She winked and Kassidy batted her away softly.

"Skiing would be fun for a change. We've never gone because of the chance of getting hurt. But I'm ready to move on."

Lauren knew how her friend felt and hoped they'd be able to help each other figure out their new lives in the coming months and years. She'd forgotten how at-home she felt with Kassidy, like she was her real sister instead of a good family friend.

"I'm sorry I've been such a bad friend," Lauren confessed. "I promise I'll do better."

"It's all in the past, Laur. We're moving on and figuring things out as we go, right?" Kassidy grinned, her white teeth beaming from the lights of the jeep.

That sounded good to Lauren. She'd begin tomorrow with a fresh start. She'd pick up her stuff from Fort Collins and rebuild and revamp until she had the life she wanted in Coldwater Creek.

CHAPTER 23

The roads were a bit icy early that next morning, but she knew she needed to get a good start so she'd have time to load everything she needed in the back of her truck. She'd planned to leave most of the furniture as she'd acquired it all from the classifieds around town over the years, some of the pieces even coming from her college apartment.

Everything would fit into the back of her dad's pickup—at least, she hoped. She'd told her dad she needed to head to Fort Collins and then she'd be back early Sunday morning, giving her enough time to be there for the dinner.

As she passed by the Silver Brook Lodge on her way out of town, all the lights were off, and she could picture Walker sleeping peacefully with Bear by his side. It was only five thirty in the morning, but tying up loose ends was her mission, and she was ready to be done with Fort Collins. As she thought back to all the times she'd had there, she wondered what had pulled her to stay.

College had been a lot of fun, especially being a small-town girl in a big city. But life after college had dragged on, mostly due to her complacency in staying with Cory. But like Kassidy said, that was all water under the bridge. She'd see where this fresh start took her and make the most of it. If nothing else, she was closer to family and had a job she already loved after one week.

And then there was Walker. She'd loved him for so long, but these feelings now were like separation anxiety. Being away from the lodge and from him was making it difficult for her to function without all the emotions swelling up inside her.

He was a good guy, and maybe after this trip, she'd have the guts to face him, to tell him she loved him and always had and see where the chips fell. Because if she could just say it out loud, that would take care of half of her inner struggle. The other half would just have to accept whatever answer came around.

A little more than eight hours later, she pulled into the driveway of her townhome. Looking at the outside, she realized this was no longer her home. She pulled out boxes she'd gotten at a nearby grocery store and carried them inside.

She began by filling the boxes with books and the knick-knacks she'd collected over the years. Her shoes and clothes all went into the suitcases she'd brought, making the house look empty after many of the personal effects had been taken away.

Making her way to the kitchen, she boxed up all the food in the kitchen and set it in the front of the pickup cab so she could donate it to a food pantry. She threw out all the perishables and made sure to clean as much as she could.

A knock sounded on the door, causing her to pause. Who would be here now? She didn't know many people in the neighborhood despite living there for three years, the problem with only associating with her ex-boyfriend's schedule and family.

Walking over to open it, she caught a glimpse of a familiar patch of light brown hair sticking up enough to see through the window at the top of the door.

She opened the door a few inches and scowled. "What do you want, Cory?"

"I made a mistake, and I'm here to fix it. Wait, what are you doing?" He stretched to see over her, taking in the boxes scattered over the floor.

"I'm moving. I'm heading back to live in Coldwater Creek." Her tone sounded flat. Even though she was over-joyed to be moving back home, she wanted Cory to leave, and the best way to do that was to not show excitement.

"Come on, you're uprooting your life because of a little argument we had? Things were good between us, and they can be again." He paused a moment. "My mother agreed to give you a raise."

Lauren snorted. "Yeah, probably a whole fifty cents so I'm no longer living on the poverty line, right? No, I'm moving back home. I've already got a job, and my boss values the skills I'm bringing with me. At least I know all that time doing your job helped to make me more marketable once I left the insurance business." She glared up at him, waiting for him to say something, anything, about their relationship.

"Well, stay here. We can get married, settle down, and have fun."

"Is that what you really want, Cory? Do you want to marry me? Because it seemed like I was just a stand-in. Have you not found the girl of your dreams in the last ten days?" Lauren folded her arms over her chest, causing him to shift from one foot to the other with discomfort.

When he didn't answer, Lauren said, her tone softer now, "Why are you really here, Cory? I know you don't love me like that, and I've come to realize that I never loved you. Just be patient. You'll find someone who your mother approves of, and you'll realize that what we had was friendship, not love."

His jaw twitched back and forth, and she wondered if he would cry. "You really don't love me?"

"No, I think I left my heart in Coldwater Creek long ago and never really got it back."

Cory nodded, disappointment crossing his face. "Well, I can't really argue that one. I guess I got so used to having you around that I took you for granted. Good luck in your new adventure." He waved as he turned away from the door, his shoulders slouched a bit as he made his way to his car.

Lauren shut the door and leaned against it, her chest heaving. She hadn't imagined saying all that to Cory, but the realization that she'd left her heart in that lodge with the retired bull rider made her want to get home as fast as possible.

Loading the boxes into the bed of the truck took about thirty minutes, and she would already have to add a tarp to the top and tie it up so nothing tumbled out on the long drive home. She was grateful her father had made her learn even little things like that, helping her with some bit of independence.

She walked back in and looked around, realizing all that was left was the furniture. She'd messaged her landlord the night before, asking if she could leave the furniture for the next tenants, and, thank goodness, they'd agreed so she didn't have to try and find some way to get it out of the building. It wouldn't have been hard if she'd told Walker where she was going and asked him to come along, but this was something she needed to do, like painting the last few brushstrokes on an almost finished painting.

She checked her phone and saw it was six in the evening. But the part that made her stomach drop was the red signal for the battery on her phone. The charger was still plugged into the outlet in her room in Coldwater Creek. She'd just have to stop and buy a car charger. It would be better to travel with a charged phone than a dead one, especially after what happened last time.

After punching the icon for her dad, she waited while it dialed. When he finally picked up, she said, "Hey, Dad. I'm all packed up. I'll leave and get a hotel in Rock Springs, and then I should be home in the morning tomorrow."

"Make sure you stop this time, then. I don't want to hear you had to be rescued because you were too stubborn to pull over." He paused a minute. "In fact, maybe you should stay there tonight and start driving in the morning. It's already nearly dark here."

"Dad, I'll be fine. And I'll listen to my body and how I feel. If I get tired, I'll pull off for the night."

"Just be safe. I don't want to lose you." His voice cracked a bit.

Lauren teared up, now understanding his caution. He'd already lost one woman in his life. He didn't want to lose another. "I'll be safe, Dad. See you tomorrow."

After hanging up, she opened a text to Walker, wanting to tell him she would be back tomorrow. She'd forgotten about his phone call the night before and hoped it hadn't been something urgent. The one-percent battery on her phone gave out before she could send the text, and the screen turned black.

She looked around the place one more time before getting into the cab. She'd run a few errands around town and go from there. As happy as she was to go, it was still hard to leave a place where eight years of her life had been spent. But new beginnings awaited her, and she wasn't about to pass that up.

CHAPTER 24

Walker tried calling Lauren again Sunday morning, wondering why she wasn't answering. This time, the call went straight to voicemail, only causing his frustration to heighten. Was she avoiding him now? He hoped not.

Everything had gotten turned around, and he just needed another chance to make things right, to not lose the person he felt alive around and who would work alongside him no matter what he was doing. She was like a ray of sunshine, and now that she'd gone and disappeared, it was like the darkest cloud had descended over him.

He'd been disappointed when Lauren hadn't called him back to go look at Christmas trees for the lodge, but now, hours away from the dinner they were to host for the Burkes and McBrides, he needed to hear her voice and her assurance that he could actually do this.

By Sunday afternoon, it had taken a few attempts to shove the thoughts away that she'd run back to Fort Collins without telling him. He wasn't prepared to live in a big city, and if that's where she wanted to be, he wouldn't know how to change her mind.

No, that wouldn't be the reason she didn't call him. She'd been so excited about working at the lodge and about being home. Kassidy had told him Lauren had gone with her to the karaoke bar on Friday, and while he was happy they had a great time, part of him wished he could have been there to enjoy it with her. Karaoke wasn't something he felt comfortable with, but he wanted to spend all the time he could with her and make it work between them. Maybe if Cara had supported him a little better, he wouldn't have felt like he was treading water for the last few months, trying not to drown.

Determined to get some answers, he got into his truck and drove to the Burke farm. He hoped someone there had answers.

When he knocked on the door, Preston answered. "Hey, Walk. What are you doing here? Aren't we supposed to meet at your place in a few hours?"

"Yeah," he said, glancing down at his watch. He had a lot he needed to prep for tonight, and he hadn't been thinking clearly. "Do you know where Lauren is? I've been trying to get ahold of her to make sure she'll be there tonight, but my calls go straight to voicemail."

Preston frowned. "I haven't talked to her in a few days. Come to think of it, I haven't seen her since Thursday. Maybe my dad knows something?"

They walked into the study where Mr. Burke was reading what looked to be a western.

"Hi, boys. What are you up to today?" he said with a smile.

"Dad, have you talked to Lauren?" Preston asked, his hands in his pockets, failing to mask the worry.

Mr. Burke nodded. "She called me yesterday. Said she was in Fort Collins—"

"She went back to Colorado?" Walker asked, feeling the frustration settle over his body like a blanket. All the fears he'd been trying to push away had come true.

Preston's hand rested on Walker's shoulder. "Walk, calm down. Maybe she had to settle something. She did talk about telling her—"

Turning on his heel, Walker stomped out of the room without waiting for the rest of the explanation. His brain wasn't going to hear it anyway. His only thought was that she'd gone back to Fort Collins, giving up on him and going back to her life there. How could he have been so blind? But then again, what had he done to prevent it?

Nothing. He'd avoided her like a bad cold the last week and snapped at her when she was trying to help him. Anger, desperation, and a lack of hope collided inside his chest, taking his breath away.

He slammed the truck door and revved the engine. He would show her. He would make sure tonight was the best dinner the restaurant ever made just so her family would make sure she knew what she was missing.

The competitive edge he hadn't felt since the last time he was in the arena surged to the surface as he raced the few miles back to the lodge. She'd believed in him and then left, just like Cara. It was time he believed in himself and made it happen. At least her advice was sound.

His focus was on the dinner that night. Once it was over and the restaurant and hotel opened on Tuesday, he'd have to find a way to mend his broken heart. But right now, he couldn't dwell on it. He'd need to use it to get through the night and assure that his company was on the right track.

CHAPTER 25

After so many errands the night before, Lauren hadn't gotten very far out of Fort Collins, maybe two hours, before she stopped for the night. The toll of driving for so long and packing and cleaning must have done something to her because despite the rock hard mattress at the motel, she slept soundly, not waking for anything.

When she did open her eyes, she saw bright coming through the small crack under the curtains. It was probably good she'd gotten some sleep, but when she looked at the clock, she realized it nearing noon, not eight like she'd guessed. With at least six hours to go until she made it to the lodge, she was going to be late for the dinner.

Lauren grabbed her things as quickly as she could and threw them into the cab of the truck. She jumped in the cab and pulled out, hoping to avoid any accidents or delays of any kind.

Just as she was about to head out, she groaned, remembering she needed to stop to buy a car charger since she'd forgotten to the night before. Once she bought it, she plugged her phone in and waited for it to charge enough to turn on. She pulled out onto the main road, hoping she could make it through the large amount of traffic for midday Sunday.

"Please turn on; please turn on," she said, pushing the side button on her phone and waiting for her carrier's logo to pop on the screen. It finally did, and she breathed a sigh of relief. Pulling up Walker's name, she pressed to dial and waited as the dial tone rang and rang, echoing in her brain.

The message came on, and just hearing his voice made her feel even more guilty, knowing she wouldn't be there like she'd said she would be.

After the beep, she rambled, probably not making much sense, but she knew she needed to get everything she could into the message.

"Walker, I'm so sorry. I'll probably be late tonight. My landlord needed me to clean things out before next week, and with the opening of everything this week, I figured Saturday would be the perfect time. I'm so sorry, and I hope you'll forgive me. I think…" She paused, her heart beating as the word "love" was on the tip of her tongue. "You are probably the greatest man alive, and I just need to make it through this traffic so I can get back to Coldwater Creek. I'm rooting that everything goes smoothly, and I'll see you when I get—" The beep sounded, cutting off her message.

After pressing end, she opened a text and sent a quick voice-to-text explanation to Kassidy, hoping she'd be able to relay the message in time. She put the phone down next to her and focused on the traffic. If only she'd set an alarm or something, maybe she wouldn't be in a mess like this.

At a complete stop on the highway, she punched Cold-water Creek into her maps app and found several long red stretches on the route. With there only being one direct route, it was still faster to go this direction, and she wanted to cry.

She'd have to try and call more of her family on the way, hoping they would help relay the message that she was doing everything she could to arrive on time.

CHAPTER 26

Once he'd made it back to the lodge from the Burkes, it seemed like Walker didn't have much time to mentally prepare himself for what was to come. Several of the workers showed up just minutes after he did, and they worked in the kitchen, chopping and peeling and preparing the courses that would be served that night.

As nervous as Walker had felt up to this point, he knew this was what he wanted, to show his family that even in something completely opposite of riding a wild animal, he could succeed and continue on, still happy with his simple life.

Potatoes were being boiled with his mother's garlic-and-salt combination, the green beans had all been cut and were now roasting, and the rolls were almost done rising, ready to be put into the warm oven to cook. The last thing to start were the steaks, as he wanted everything to come out as warm as possible. Cooking for a group of fourteen people seemed overwhelming, but as everyone fell into their places and routines, getting things plated at the same time would be the challenge.

One of the wait staff had been assigned to welcome and seat the families, and he was grateful for that much, as their chatter caused his insides to flip and twist like a gymnastic routine.

At half past five, he was able to finish all the food, making sure to get it all set up for the waiters to take out to the group. He was proud of the looks of it all. The two women plating had done a great job with the presentation of the food. Blowing out a breath, he just hoped his guests liked it.

As he thanked everyone on the team, he was amazed that even though he'd known some of these people since he was a kid, seeing them in their element had changed his view of them for the better.

"You did pretty well, Walker. Are you sure you've never done any actual cooking?" Paula, one of the platers asked.

"To be honest, how hard is it to mess up meat and potatoes?" Walker chuckled, and she joined in. "I guess we'll see what it's like when we make several different foods all at once."

"As long as you delegate like you did tonight, you'll be fine. It's the chefs that think they know it all and try to do it all that end up having the worst backup of food." She nodded at him and walked away.

He'd promised the crew they'd be able to leave without the cleanup, knowing they'd have plenty in the weeks to come. It was the least he could do until the company was making money and he could compensate them for tonight.

Moving out to his family and the Burkes, he smiled and asked, "What did you think?"

"Everything was delicious," his mother said, grinning at him. "Someone is trying to use my garlic mashed potatoes on his menu."

"It's a family favorite, and you all loved it, right?" He

looked around the table for confirmation, grateful that most of the heads were nodding.

Mr. Burke rested his hands on this stomach, leaning back in his seat. "Walker, what you've done with this place puts the old lodge to shame. The craftsmanship, the attention to detail…well done."

Walker smiled, feeling a sliver of pride at his comments. But for some reason, they didn't mean as much as someone else's. A certain girl with long hair and piercing green eyes. But she hadn't made it, and his frustration drove him to shake any thought of her away.

"What's for dessert?" Colter asked, looking ready to eat an entire pie.

Walker opened his mouth, realizing it had been too easy and he'd forgotten to prepare something for dessert. "Um, I have some Oreos out back you can have. I don't really have a dessert menu ready yet."

The group stood slowly, and his mother walked over. "Don't worry, dear. If you need to come look through my recipes to figure out some desserts, you can do that tomorrow." She kissed his cheek.

He gave her a grateful smile. "Thanks, Mom. I'll have to do that. It would be even better if you somehow had recipes for the desserts from the old lodge." He was hoping beyond hope with that request.

"You never know what's in my cookbook treasure trove."

"Thanks, Mom."

The families filed out, thanking him for the meal, and Colter disappeared into the kitchen, only to bring back the package of Oreos a minute later. When Walker raised an eyebrow, he said, "What? You said you had some, and I already ate all the goodies Mom made for the weekend."

"You're good. Take it with you."

As the last person left the lodge, the silence became deafening. He was exhausted, and all he wanted to do was sleep, but with the dishes in the sink, he knew he'd need to get them cleaned before all the stuck-on foods became hard.

Trudging into the kitchen, he turned on some music to drown out the silence and help him focus on the dishes. It was going to be a long night, and as mad as he was about Lauren not coming, he wished she was there by his side. But things were so messed up that the chances of that happening were slim to none.

CHAPTER 27

*L*auren was ready to burn every orange cone she saw after driving on the road, hating that they'd decided to do a bunch of construction on a two-lane highway on a Sunday. She was already late for the five o'clock dinner, but she had a small chance of making it for the end. At least some appearance would be better than none.

She'd tried dialing everyone's phone number she had, but none of them had picked up, probably enjoying the meal Walker was preparing for them.

She glanced at the clock on her dash, seeing it was nearly nine o'clock as she pulled into the driveway of Silver Brook Lodge. She enjoyed the view of the place just as much as she had when she'd passed by it the day before.

Lights were still on, but the only car in the parking lot was Walker's. Her hopes sank. She'd have to talk to Walker and hopefully smooth things over.

She knocked on the front door a few times and then opened it, walking inside. There was no sign of Walker in the great room, but a faint sound of music made her change course toward the kitchen.

"Knock, knock." She pretended to tap on an invisible door.

Walker stood in front of the large sink, the load of dirty dishes at the side of him towering. He stopped scrubbing and turned slowly. When he saw her standing there, she'd hoped to find some kind of excitement in his expression or the least bit of hope that he felt the same as she did. But his face was a serene mask, no emotion coming through at all.

"You're late." He turned back and resumed his washing, the muscles in his back tensing.

"I know, and I'm so incredibly sorry. There was traffic and construction, and every other thing that could go wrong did today. Did it go well?" Her voice sounded much higher than she wanted it to, but she hoped he didn't hear the difference.

"The dinner went well, yes. But I forgot about dessert. What kind of fancy steakhouse doesn't have a dessert menu?"

Lauren frowned, surprised by the admission. "That's something we still have time to come up with. It will be fine."

"I thought you were staying in Fort Collins." His words were clipped, and Lauren just wanted to go back to the relationship they'd had a week ago.

"I went back to clean out my townhouse. I knew with everything happening this next week that I wouldn't get a chance to, and I wanted to just be done—"

Walker turned around, his eyes avoiding hers. "Look, it's been a really long day. There's still a lot to get ready before Tuesday, and I'm really tired."

Lauren's mouth dropped open a bit, shocked at his words. "Uh, okay. Yeah, I'll leave you alone. Or could you use some help with those dishes?"

He raised both hands. "I'll be fine. Just go home."

Taking that as a signal, she nodded, feeling the shame as

she walked through the door. She'd screwed things up worse than she'd imagined.

Her heart sank as she slipped into the cab of her dad's truck. The insurance company had come back, saying her car had been totaled, but the payoff she'd be getting wasn't enough for a down payment on anything new or used. She'd hoped she would be able to figure something out once the lodge was making money. But would Walker want to see her? He wasn't saying she was fired by sending her home, right?

It didn't matter. She was going to show up the next day and work to make sure she made up for today's mistake.

* * *

NOT HAVING GOTTEN MUCH REST the night before, Lauren had made a list of all the things she needed to get done in the next day and a half. Finishing up the Christmas decorations in the lodge was on the list, but the priority was getting the word out about the opening of the restaurant Tuesday night. She would work to call several of the locals, hoping that by getting the opening night off to a great start, Walker would forgive her for missing out on the party the night before.

One of the main things she'd put off over the past week was the pictures in the rooms and the ones over the mantle. She knew she didn't have time to get any fancy frames, but she'd need to work fast if she was going to have every last element in place before people showed up.

After jumping in the shower, she dressed and pulled her hair back, knowing that today was going to be hectic and to bother with leaving it down would be a hassle. She was grateful for the extended amount of clothing she had as she pulled on a forest-green sweater and some jeans.

As soon as eight o'clock rolled around, she was dialing numbers, knowing that time was of the essence.

Her first call was to the print shop in Jackson Hole. They would be her best bet for getting the prints done quickly.

"Hi, Janet," Lauren said once the woman came on the line. "I'm looking to get several large prints made as a surprise for a friend. Would there be a possibility you can get those done by this afternoon? I will pay any expedited fee you need."

"Let me see what I have in our system. Do you know what sizes you would need?" the woman asked, breathing heavily into the phone.

Lauren had already worked out the details and had a list for each of the rooms. She read off the sizes and number of each to the woman, hoping they would be able to make it happen.

After several minutes, the woman said, "We should be able to accommodate you. Because it will be a one-day print on all of these, we will need to charge you an extra five hundred dollars."

Lauren gulped. This project would probably eat up every bit of her savings, but she'd find a way to build it back again. "Okay, that will work. I'll send those prints over by email now with the specified sizes on them. What time can I come pick them up?"

"We close at six, so if you can be here by 5:30, we should have everything done for you."

Lauren thanked the woman and hung up, still trying to breathe from the thought of the amount. Checking her bank account, she'd have about a thousand dollars left over. Was it worth it to spend that money on these pictures? Something inside her nudged her forward, and she knew she had to do it. No matter how Walker felt about her, she loved him.

The words rolled over her tongue, and little sparks of excitement broke out all over her. She would just have to find someone who could make the frames and quickly. Since it was a lodge, a simple aged wood frame would be perfect to show off the amazing colors and light in the shots Colter had taken.

But who could build something that quickly? She tapped her finger against her lips. She went through her family, shaking her head as each of her brothers' faces popped into her mind. Then she thought about Walker's family. Easton was too busy taking care of the ranch, fixing everything he hadn't had time to fix while coaching during Coldwater Creek's high school football season.

Colter took pictures, but Hunter was the one who'd been fiddling with wood since he was young, scavenging it from anywhere he could find it and building things. He would be her best bet.

Lauren pulled up Kassidy's number and dialed, tapping her leg in the hopes that her friend would answer. To get twenty-five frames made in thirty-six hours was going to be a feat, but she'd run over and do her best to help if that would pull this whole plan together.

"Hey, Laur. What are you up to today? We missed you last night." Her voice had that questioning curiosity so prevalent to Kassidy, and Lauren shook it off.

"Yeah, I got stuck in some traffic coming back from Fort Collins. Did you not get my text?"

"No, nothing came through last night. I'm just glad you're okay. I was worried when you weren't at the dinner and Walker was too agitated to talk. I can only imagine he was worried and mad you weren't there."

Lauren winced. She recalled his face from the night before and pushed it out of her mind before she lost all hope of showing him how much she cared. "Can I get Hunter's number? I have a big project I need to see if he'll do for me by tomorrow."

"Sure, I'll text it over. Anything I can help with?"

Lauren looked at her list. "I think that's about it for now.

Depending on his answer, I might need your help with it too." She thought for a moment. "If you have time to drive to Jackson with me tonight, I would appreciate the company."

"What's in Jackson?"

"I'm getting those pictures of Colter's printed, and I was hoping Hunter could help make the frames for them. I don't know if Walker will ever forgive me for not showing up last night, but I hope this can be some sort of a peace offering."

Silence caused Lauren to pause, and she pulled her phone away to see if she still had service. The call was still connected, and Kassidy finally spoke. "You love him, don't you?"

Hearing it from her best friend's mouth put things into perspective, causing a type of resolve to build inside her. "I do. And I might end up heartbroken for Christmas, but I hope this shows just how much he means to me. Dreams and all."

"I hope he listens. If he doesn't, he's passing up the greatest thing that's ever happened to him."

Lauren thanked her and hung up. She didn't have time to dwell on that now. She needed to get moving in order to have everything ready for showtime tomorrow.

CHAPTER 28

Walker moved slower than normal while getting up on Tuesday morning, trying to work the sore muscles in his shoulders and back from the last week of repairs and tension. It had taken longer than he wanted to fall asleep, and every time he closed his eyes, he could see the disappointment on Lauren's face after he'd told her to leave.

He'd been so angry at the thought of her leaving that he couldn't get past it even when she showed up, telling him she was staying in Coldwater Creek. He just wished she'd said something, anything. Because everything he'd gone through over the past few days felt a lot like what he'd gone through before Cara had officially broken things off. But this time, he knew there was no hope of his heart staying intact if it were to happen with Lauren.

He'd seen a voicemail on his phone the day before, but he hadn't had time to listen to it as he'd gone to his parents' home in search of easy but delicious dessert recipes. His mother had worked with him to have six different options. He'd gotten that put onto the menu and sent to the printer, trashing the copies he'd received the Friday before.

Maybe he should postpone the opening day. So many things seemed to be pulling at his attention, and he wasn't sure if everything would be finished by that night. He'd heard Lauren working in the lodge the day before, and it seemed like the Christmas décor was ready at the lodge. Everything except a Christmas tree. It was too late to get one before tonight, but he'd have to make a trip to the mountains this weekend. He knew he'd get enough questions from guests asking why he didn't have a tree next to the large windows in the great room.

Shaking off the doubts, he got out of bed, knowing he'd have to pick up the food order from the butcher and the grocer today. If he did that this morning, he would have plenty of time to make sure he had everything he needed. But would anyone show up?

He'd done a lot by word of mouth, and he knew his family was telling everyone about the opening of the new restaurant, but he mentally kicked himself. Why hadn't he thought to get all that done and ready to go out while he'd been snowed in?

He knew why. Those eyes that haunted him, that pulled him in and held his interest. But she was just like Cara. Could he count on her to be there for the difficult moments of his life?

While dressing, he pressed the voicemail button and entered his code, putting it on speaker so he could hear it in his closet. After the automated voice told him the details of the call, he heard Lauren's voice.

At first, anger filled him, but then everything began to click, and he realized what a fool he'd been.

"You are probably the greatest man alive, and I just need to make it through this traffic so I can get back to Coldwater Creek. I'm rooting everything goes smoothly, and I'll see you when I get—" and then a beep sounded, ending the message.

He pressed the button to listen to it again, this time sitting on the edge of his bed. He didn't know how she really felt about him, but piecing together the message with the look of hope and remorse on her face Sunday evening, he knew it was worth taking a chance on her. It wasn't easy to deny his feelings for her, and he just hoped he wasn't too late to tell her.

He dialed her number, hoping she would answer. But after several rings, it went straight to voicemail. He dialed Kassidy next and finally heard her voice when he was sure the message would come on.

"What's up, Walker? Are you all ready for tonight?" Kassidy sounded breathless like she'd been running.

"It will be. Are you at the bank today?"

"No, I took the day off. I have a, uh, lot to catch up on for, um, this project I'm working on, so I need to get back to it. Was there something you needed?"

Walker ran his hand through his hair, wondering if he should even hint to his sister that he loved her best friend. But Lauren was also his employee. He could ask about her without any certain suspicions.

"Have you seen Lauren? I wasn't sure what time she was coming in today, but she didn't pick up my call."

"She told me she'd be busy getting more Christmas decorations for the lodge." Kassidy's words sounded rehearsed, and Walker wondered what would cause that.

"Okay, well, if you do see her, tell her to give me a call." He hung up, buttoning the last of his shirt and walking out to grab his coat.

"Stay here, Bear. I'll be back in a bit with all the food." He just hoped he'd have enough room to make it in one trip with his pickup. After this first week, he'd need to look into some type of delivery service so he didn't have to worry about things like that.

He took one more glance around the lodge, seeing little touches of Lauren everywhere. They made him smile, and the urge to tell her how he felt rose within him. Some way or another, he would find a moment alone with her and tell her. He may as well know now if she reciprocated his feelings or not, just so he could move on if she didn't.

But he couldn't help but hope she felt the same.

CHAPTER 29

Lauren crumpled into a heap on the old couch out in the McBride's workshop. She'd gotten only a few hours of sleep between driving up to Jackson and back and then helping Hunter with the frames. She'd worked to help him measure things out, making the cutting go by much faster, but the clock was ticking, and she just hoped she'd be able to pull it off.

"These look amazing," Kassidy said, coming through the door. She'd helped a bit the night before but had done some of the errands Lauren had begged her to do, allowing Lauren to help out on this huge task she'd asked of one of Walker's twin brothers.

"Don't they? How many have we done, Hunter?"

A compressed staple gun went off. "This is number twenty-three out of twenty-five. We're almost there." He gave them a quick glance before focusing on the next part of the frame. There were several different sizes. Lauren just hoped they'd done them all correctly.

"Will you help me put the prints in the frames? We'll have to get Mr. Turner down at the glass company to cut us some after the holidays. I would hate to ruin any of these prints." Lauren pulled out one picture of a field, the large mountains looming in the background. It was just barely sunup, and the light from the first rays of sun made the scene look magical.

Kassidy stood next to her, *ooh*ing and *ahh*ing about each one as they settled them into the frames. Too bad Lauren hadn't acted on this plan the day she and Kassidy had talked about it. She could have had them completely finished. But then again, her bank account would be in the red.

Nerves welled up in her. What if Walker didn't like them? What if he was really done with her? What would she do?

She pushed those thoughts away, being only hours away from the opening of the Silver Brook Lodge and Restaurant. She wasn't going to derail all the work everyone had already put in because of a few doubts. If anything, this just bettered the look of the lodge—and hopefully boosted Colter's name as a photographer.

"Walker is going to love these. Sometimes I wonder how I'm related to all these siblings with such talent." Kassidy's tone soured, and her face puckered like she'd just tasted a lemon.

"What are you talking about? You're just as talented as the rest of the McBrides. We just don't tell you so you won't get a big head." Lauren grinned at her and then jumped out of the way to avoid a swing to the shoulder.

Hunter laughed so hard that the two of them turned to look at him. "That was a good one, Lauren. It's good to have you back in Coldwater Creek."

Lauren smiled. She had felt more at home than ever these past couple of weeks, and she just hoped it continued. Whether or not she and Walker were together, she just hoped he would let her keep her job.

Thinking about it more, would she survive seeing him day in and day out, knowing how she felt about him and then seeing him date some other faceless woman? She may as well get a job at the grocery store if she was going to torture herself.

Breathing out slowly, she ticked off the mental list. All she needed to get done now was to put ribbons around each of the framed prints and get them over to the lodge without any damage. And without Walker knowing anything about it.

CHAPTER 30

Four o'clock came, and Walker's stomach was a giant ball of nerves. He hadn't seen any of his family all day, which was unusual since at least one of them had stopped by every day since the snow had been cleared from the roads. This was his big day. Was everyone going to disappoint him?

He couldn't remember how many times he'd checked his phone, hoping to see something from Lauren, but he should've known better. He was the reason she'd left, and he was the reason she'd been avoiding him at all costs. What would help him convince her that he was sorry?

Well, it would be nice to see her first, to actually talk to her face-to-face, even though those emerald eyes of hers would probably jumble every word in his brain.

The cooking and wait staff had shown up, and all of them were preparing for opening night. Several of the ones in the kitchen were chopping and prepping different ingredients, all of which would make it easier to get the food cooked and out to the guests in a reasonable time frame. Walker tried to take his mind off Lauren by making sure several of the desserts he'd made earlier that day had set.

A door swung open and sounded like it hit a wall, causing Walker to investigate. Preston stood in the doorway, bundled up in what looked like every piece of snow clothes he owned.

"What are you doing?" Walker asked, more curious than annoyed.

"I need you to, um, come help me check out my, uh, truck. It's out back, and it's been acting kind of funny." Preston shifted from one foot to the other, looking more uncomfortable than ever.

Shaking his head and frowning, Walker said, "Preston, you have a brother who's a mechanic. I have to help with the prep in the kitchen. Can't you go ask Seth?"

Preston's eyebrows merged into one long dark caterpillar. "Well, uh, he's really busy picking up some girl to bring to dinner tonight, so I can't right now. And I have to go pick up a few other people. Just help me out, man."

Knowing his friend wouldn't leave him alone until he did it, Walker took off his apron and slung his coat over his shoulders, wondering what could have prompted such an awkward display of acting.

Slapping Preston on the shoulder, he said, "Just don't quit your day job." He grinned, and Preston scowled at him as they walked outside.

"The things I do for my sister," Preston muttered under his breath.

Walker stopped. What could that mean?

"I've been meaning to ask you," his best friend said, causing Walker's heart to skip a beat. "Is there anything going on between you two?"

Walker gulped, trying to swallow the lump of guilt that had formed in his throat. "Well, uh, Preston, I'm not sure." He rubbed at the back of his neck, suddenly sweating in the chilly air. Telling himself he needed to get this over with, he looked into his friend's eyes and said, "I love your sister, Preston. You probably shouldn't be the first one to hear that, but it's the best way I know how to tell you. I've watched you torture and scare off guys she's dated over the years, but I know I can withstand everything you've done to them up to this point. I'm not sure if she feels the same, and that's why I've held back from telling you."

Preston's jaw twitched back and forth a bit, causing Walker's stomach to clench in anticipation of his reaction. A half-smile surfaced, and Preston hit him on the shoulder. "It's about dang time you figured that out. I always knew you two would be good together, especially when she would sit and listen to you talk about whatever problems you had going on. Sometimes for what felt like forever."

"Wait? You're okay with it?" Walker wasn't sure how to feel, but his mind spun with the relief that he wasn't going to lose his best friend over this.

"You're a million times better for her than that Cory guy, and I think she knows it. Tell her how you feel, and go from there."

* * *

Fifteen minutes later, Walker walked back inside, anxious about helping out in the kitchen. Why he'd let his friend talk him into something ridiculous on one of the biggest nights of his life, he'd never know. But at least he finally had Preston's blessing on a relationship with Lauren, if he could salvage one. He threw his coat on the rack and changed out his snow boots for tennis shoes before heading down the hall, tying his apron around his waist as he walked.

What he found in the great room caused him to stop in

his tracks. There were at least thirty to forty people standing there, and only a couple of them were his family.

"What are you all doing here?" he asked, trying to find someone who would speak up.

"We're here for the restaurant opening and to congratulate you on rebuilding the lodge," one woman at the front of the group said. She looked somewhat familiar, but he wasn't sure of her name.

Kassidy pushed her way to the front and, with hands on hips, said, "We've got a big surprise for you."

At her words, the crowd parted, and leaning against his recliner chair were stacks of wood. Moving forward, he walked around to find amazing pictures of the Coldwater Creek valley, some of the spots looking more recognizable than others.

"These are amazing," he said, pulling another frame toward him. His family's ranch at dusk stared back at him, causing emotion to rise to his throat. "Who did these?"

"Colter took the pictures. Hunter and Lauren put together the frames. She's put in an order for the glass of each one, but it won't be done until right before Christmas." Kassidy grinned at him, and when she raised her eyebrows, he knew she was expecting a response.

Walker stood, looking through the crowd. Only a few whispers could be heard in the room. No sight of the girl his heart belonged to.

"Where is Lauren?" he asked, feeling impatience surge within him. He needed to talk to her now, to tell her how much he loved her and that this gift was one of the best things he'd ever been given.

"She said something about running to the kitchen."

Walker turned and left without hesitation, hoping the crowd would understand his sudden departure. He burst through the kitchen doors, pulling the attention of everyone except one form with her back to him. Her long ponytail reached the middle of her back, and she looked like she was trying to cut something.

"What are you doing in here?" His tone came out gruffer than he'd wanted, but it had the effect of turning the rest of the staff back to what they'd been doing.

Lauren stilled, her breathing slower as the silence stretched on.

She finally turned around, a potato and a peeler in her hand. "Well, I missed out on helping cook for the first meal. I didn't want to miss out on opening night." Her smile was small, hesitant, as if waiting for his reaction.

The look on her face was innocent and almost hopeful. Walker just hoped it meant what he wanted it to. That she felt the same way he did.

He maneuvered around the island to stand before her, placing his hands on her upper arms. Her shoulders relaxed somewhat.

"You made all those pictures for me?" he asked, his voice quiet. Emotion had finally taken over, and he was finding it hard to swallow around the mound that had formed in his throat.

Lauren's eyes glistened. "Yes." It seemed like she wanted to say more, but she stopped, her eyes dancing around as they studied his face.

"Why? Why go to the effort of all that?"

One corner of her mouth ticked up, and she shrugged. "I just wanted you to know that I care about you and that I want things to work out for you and the lodge. I know it was a huge risk, but you've come so far. And I'd hoped you would forgive me for missing dinner the other night."

Walker reached up and caressed her cheek with the back of his hand. "And I hope you'll forgive me for being a jerk that night…and on Friday. I should have let you explain. I was just worried you were leaving before everything happened, that you realized you couldn't work here or something."

Lauren's full smile returned. "Are you kidding? This is the place I feel fulfilled and like my job actually matters."

Walker took a step forward, taking in a breath as he did so. He opened his mouth to reply, but someone called out, "One hour to opening!" and several of the staff hurried around them.

Reaching down, he took Lauren's hand, leading her out to the back porch. It was chilly, but he didn't have much time and knew that if he waited, he'd never get this out.

"I'm sorry about everything, Lauren. I love you, and I'm sorry I hurt you. Will you please forgive me?" He met her gaze and felt as if fireworks had been set off in his heart.

"You love me?" she asked, blinking several times.

Panic spread across his chest. From the surprise on her face, she was either surprised by his admission or trying her best to find a way to turn him down.

Looking down at their joined hands, Walker nodded before looking up again. "Yes. There is so much good to you, and thinking you were moving back to Fort Collins crushed me. I thought I'd lost you."

Lauren let go of his hand and lifted her arms behind his neck. She leaned forward and whispered, "I love you too. I always have."

Walker paused, hoping he hadn't just imagined the words. When she leaned back enough for him to see her face, he leaned in, pressing his lips to hers softly. The sensations he'd always felt when he touched her seemed magnified, like electricity finding conducive material. He wrapped his arms around her back and pulled her to him, enjoying the warmth of her lips against the cold wind.

When they finally broke apart, he leaned his forehead

against hers. "I have to get back to the kitchen. You don't have to leave early tonight, do you?"

She shook her head. "I'm all yours. Let me help out in the kitchen."

"Why don't you make Preston hang all the frames? That can be his payback for keeping me out in the cold so long."

Lauren smiled, reached up, and gave him a peck on the lips before turning and heading back inside. Whatever he'd done to deserve a girl like her, Walker didn't know. But the excitement of a future together was something he looked forward to more than ever.

EPILOGUE

Two weeks later, the lodge and restaurant were booked nearly every night. Lauren had created several systems and had worked with an online tech guy to get as much automated on the website as possible, which helped cut down on all the extra phone calls and work she had to do.

Walker had been getting great reviews for his cooking, and while he loved it, he'd still reached out to a few other chefs who would be able to start after the first of the year, allowing him to take a few nights off here and there.

They'd gone up the mountain the weekend after opening and cut down the perfect Christmas tree for the great room.

Lauren sat on the couch across from it, mesmerized by the twinkling lights and beautiful decorations. It was Christmas Eve, and with the McBride family party over for the night, she'd stayed to hang out at the lodge for a bit before heading home.

"Your hot chocolate, m'lady," Walker said, coming up behind her.

She grinned, grateful for this change in her life. If only

she'd known how much real love could change her world, she would have given up on Cory after the first month of dating.

Walker sat down and snuggled next to her, draping his arm over her shoulders. She took the warm mug and sipped at the chocolate, savoring the perfect amount of flavor.

"I don't know how you make this so well every time, but I'll never get sick of it." She beamed up at him and blew a little into the cup, hoping not to burn her taste buds.

"Secret family recipe." Walker winked.

They sat in silence for several moments, and she relished this picture-perfect moment. She knew there were bound to be ups and downs in their relationship, but she was content in that moment, just basking in the warmth of the wood stove and the Christmas lights.

"Did you have fun at the party?" Lauren could feel Walker's deep voice rumble against her cheek as he said it.

She sat up a bit. "I loved it. Your brothers crack me up with their acting skills." She recalled the scene from one of the guessing games they'd played with his family. The twins' gestures were always over the top, but it worked, helping their team win.

"They definitely keep life interesting. Do you want one of your presents early?" he asked, trying to keep back a grin.

"One? I thought we weren't doing gifts, Walker McBride." She tried to make her voice sound frustrated, but she couldn't stay mad at him long with the cockeyed smile he was flashing her now.

"I never really agreed to that," he said, chuckling.

Rolling her eyes, Lauren shook her head. What was she going to do with him?

Walker stood and walked toward the Christmas tree. She watched as he searched several sections of the tree and then found what he wanted. With his hands behind his back, he took a few steps toward her.

"Close your eyes."

Lauren listened and closed her eyes, holding out her hands. He set something on her palm, light and square.

"Can I open them now?"

"Yes." The word came out more as a whisper, and when she opened her eyes, he was kneeling in front of her, looking at the present like it might explode.

She unwrapped it to reveal a velvet box. She gasped, doing her best to keep her heart rate down as her mind raced. Was this what she thought it was?

Opening the lid, there sat a perfect round diamond in a silver band. She glanced up at Walker, placing her hand over her mouth.

"Lauren Michelle Burke, I know we haven't been dating long, but with knowing you my whole life and after all the time we've spent together, I've never been more sure about anything in my life. Would you be my wife?"

Tears formed in the corners of her eyes, and she shifted forward to wrap her arms around his neck. "Yes!" She leaned down and kissed him, feeling as though she might fly from all the excitement bubbling up within her.

As they pulled back, she grinned.

"What's so funny?" he asked.

"I don't know how many times I wrote Lauren McBride on my notebooks in school, dreaming of a day like this. You've made my dreams come true, Walker."

"And I don't want to ever be without you, Lauren."

She pulled him back onto the couch and kissed him, grateful for the broken, mixed-up road it had taken to get here.

* * *

Continue Easton & Natalie's story in
Love in the Lights

* * *

Thank you for reading *Love in a Blizzard!* If you enjoyed it, I would love to see a review from you. You can also subscribe to Britney's newsletter here:
Subscribe to Britney's List

Loving His Reporter Girl

* * *

Join Britney's newsletter

Get the latest updates on new releases and other fun tidbits!

Britney Mills was born in Utah but parts of her heart lie in Boston, Washington D.C. and Germany. Her love of writing began with the third grade book her teacher assigned her to write and she spent hours hidden behind her mother's couch writing pages and pages about knights and castles. Now she writes about romance. Go figure.

When she's not mothering her five small children, writing or reading, she's probably out playing a sport, going on a hike, or binge watching a murder mystery series. The way to her heart is through homemade chocolate chip cookies and five minutes peace.